The White Steamship

By the same author

FAREWELL, GUL'SARY!

The White Steamship

by
CHINGIZ AITMATOV

Translated from the Russian
by
Tatyana and George Feifer

HODDER AND STOUGHTON
LONDON · SYDNEY · AUCKLAND · TORONTO

English translation copyright © 1972 by Hodder and Stoughton Ltd. Afterword copyright © 1972 by Tatyana and George Feifer. First printed 1972. ISBN 0 340 15996 0. All rights reserved. No part of this publication may be reproduced or transmitted in any form or by any means, electronic or mechanical, including photocopy, recording, or any information storage and retrieval system, without permission in writing from the publisher. Printed in Great Britain for Hodder and Stoughton Limited, St. Paul's House, Warwick Lane, London EC4P 4AH by Ebenezer Baylis and Son Limited, The Trinity Press, Worcester, and London.

Publisher's Note

The Afterword by the translators, p. 167, explores for the English-speaking reader the place of Chingiz Aitmatov in contemporary Russian literature and of *The White Steamship* among his published works.

I

He had two tales. One was his own, about which no one knew. The other was the one his grandfather used to tell. Then neither remained. Which is the heart of the matter.

That year he'd turned seven and was going on eight.

First a briefcase was bought. A black leatherette briefcase with shiny metal clips which slipped under catches. With a side pocket for odds and ends. In short, an extraordinary, wholly ordinary schoolboy's briefcase. You might say that everything began with this.

Grandfather bought it in a mobile shop. A kind of general store on wheels which made the rounds of the mountain cattle breeders with its goods, sometimes dropping in on them in the San-Tash canyon.

From there, beyond the cordon, the mountain forest preserve climbed along gorges and ravines to the upper reaches. In all, three families were settled in the cordon. Still, from time to time, the mobile shop called on the foresters too.

The only lad in all the three households, he was always first to spy the mobile shop.

"It's coming!" he'd cry, dashing to doors and windows. "The motor-market's coming!"

The twin ruts of road wound their way here from the banks of the Issik-Kul, keeping to gorges and the river bank in its route over rocks and pits. It wasn't particularly easy to drive on such a road. Having reached Guard Mountain, the road climbed from the bottom of the pass to the slope, and from there slowly descended along a steep, bald incline to the foresters' houses. Guard Mountain was very close: in summer, the lad sprinted there almost every day to survey the lake through binoculars. And from there, everything on the road was always as easy to see as if on your palm: people on foot and on horses – and, of course, the lorry.

This time – which took place during a hot summer – the lad was swimming in his little river pond, from where he saw the dust kicked up by the lorry coming down the slope. The pond was on the edge of a kind of shallow in the river, laid out along the pebbly bank. Grandfather had constructed it with rocks. If it weren't for the little pool, who knows: perhaps the lad would have lost his life long ago. And as old grandma used to say, the river would have washed him clean to the bones and flushed him straight into the Issik-Kul, where fish and all kinds of underwater creatures would have probed his remains. And no one would take the trouble to search or grieve for him – because there's no sense in poking into the water, and because he'd be nobody's great loss. So far this hadn't happened. And if it did, who knows – maybe old grandma really wouldn't rush to save him. Had he been her own blood, perhaps; but as she said, he was somebody else's. And somebody else's means always somebody else's, however much you feed him and however long you pick up after him. Somebody else's ... but what if he didn't want to be somebody else's? And why was he the one who had to be considered somebody else's? Maybe not he but old grandma herself was somebody else's?

But this comes later—and the story of grandfather's pond belongs later too...

And so he spied the mobile shop that day; it was descending from the mountain, followed by a trail of dust along the road. He felt a wave of happiness, as if he knew that the briefcase would be bought for him. He leapt out of the water instantly, quickly pulled his trousers over his skinny hips and, still wet and blue—for the river was cold—dashed down the trail to the house to be the first to herald the mobile shop's arrival.

The lad ran quickly, hopping over bushes and around the boulders he wasn't able to jump. He didn't dally anywhere, even for a second—not near the high grass, not near the rocks, although he knew that they were far from ordinary. They could feel insulted and even trip people. "The motor-market's arrived. I'll come back later," he tossed off while rushing past 'lying camel', as he called a ginger, hunch-backed piece of granite sunk into the earth up to its chest.

Ordinarily, the lad wouldn't pass without patting his 'camel' on its hump. He patted him in the manner of an animal's master, like grandfather his short-tailed gelding— just a casual, off-handed tap as if to say, "You wait around, I'm off to take care of something near by." He had a boulder called 'saddle'—half white and half black, a skewbald rock with a saddle-like hollow on which you could mount, as on a horse. There was also a 'wolf' rock which looked very much like a real wolf—tawnyish and flecked with grey, with powerful withers and weighty brows. He would steal up to him on all fours and take aim. But his favourite rock was the 'tank', an indestructible boulder on the very bank of the river, which was hollowed away by the current. Any second now the 'tank' would charge from the bank and plunge on, and the river would seethe, boiling with whitecaps. That's the way tanks move in the cinema, after all: down the bank and into the water—forward! The lad rarely saw films and therefore stoutly remembered what he saw. Grandfather sometimes drove his grandson to the cinema at the state bloodstock farm in the neighbouring glen, on the other side of the mountain. Which is why the 'tank' appeared on the bank, always on the ready to dart across the river. There were other rocks too, 'good' and 'bad' rocks, even 'cunning' and 'stupid'.

Among the plants too, there were 'favourites', 'brave ones' and others who were 'bashful' or 'wicked'. The stinging burdock, for example, was enemy number one. The lad crossed swords with it a dozen times a day. But the end of this war was not in sight: the burdock kept growing and multiplying. And there was the bindweed – which, although just a weed too, had the smartest and happiest flowers of all. They were better than all the others at greeting the sun in the morning. The other grasses understood nothing whatever: morning or evening, it was all the same to them. But all the bindweed needed was a bit of warming by the sun's rays and it opened its eyes and laughed. First one eye, then a second, and finally all the bindweed's blossoms uncurled. White, light blue, lilac, all kinds ... and if you sat near them and stayed absolutely still, it seemed as if, just after awakening, they were whispering inaudibly about something. But the ants knew all about it. They ran all over the bindweed in the morning, screwing up their eyes in the sunshine and listening to what the flowers were saying to one another. Maybe they were telling their dreams?

Later, usually around noon, the lad liked to make his way into the thickets of stalky shiraljins. The shiraljins were very tall and had no flowers, but gave off a strong fragrance; they grew in bunches, tight little clusters that let no other plants near. Shiraljins were loyal friends. Especially when there was some kind of hurt and you felt like crying so that no one could see, the shiraljins were the best place to take cover. They smelled like the entrance to a pine forest. It was hot and peaceful in the shiraljins, and the main thing was, they didn't block the sky. The best way was to lie on your back and look into the sky. At first you could hardly make out anything through the tears. Then some clouds would float by and they'd become anything you'd want them to up there. The clouds knew that things weren't so good with you, that you wanted to run away somewhere, or fly away so that nobody would find you, and then everybody would sigh and pine after you: the boy's disappeared, they'd say, and where will we find him now? ... And so that this wouldn't happen, so that you didn't disappear anywhere, so that you lay there quietly and gazed at the clouds, they'd turn into anything you wanted. From one and the same cloud you could get all kinds of different things. You just had to figure out what the clouds were depicting.

It was peaceful in the shiraljins, and they didn't block the sky. That's the kind they were, the shiraljins, with their smell of hot pine trees ...

And he knew all matter of other things about the grasses. To the silvery feather-grass which grew in the marshy meadow, he was condescending. They were funny ones, those feather-grasses. Feather-brained. Their delicate, silky whisks couldn't live without wind. They just waited around for it, and whichever way it blew, that's the way they'd bow. They all bowed together, the whole meadow as if by command. And if it rained or a storm started up, the feather-grass didn't know where to seek shelter. If they'd had legs, they'd run away, probably just following their own noses ... But they only pretended this. As soon as the storm calmed down, the empty-headed feather-grasses were again at the wind's command—wherever it blew, they bowed ...

Alone, without friends, the little shaver lived in the world of these guileless things which surrounded him, and only the mobile shop could make him forget everything and run headlong for it. Nobody needed to tell him: the mobile shop wasn't a collection of stones or some species of grass. It had just about everything under the sun, that mobile shop!

When the lad had run down to his house, the mobile shop was already approaching the yard behind the houses. The houses in the cordon faced the river; the front yards fused into an easy slope which descended straight to the bank, and on the other side of the river, directly from the bank hollowed away by the current, a steep forest rose directly into the mountains. Thus there was only one approach to the cordon, from behind the houses. Had the lad not dashed back in time, no one would have known that the mobile shop was already there.

At that hour, none of the men were about; they'd all gone off early in the morning. The women were at their household chores. But at this moment, he cried piercingly, running up to the open doors.

"It's arrived! The motor-market's arrived!"

The women were thrown into a flutter. They rushed to unearth the money they'd laid aside. And dashed out, one overtaking the other. Even old grandma praised him.

"That's our little sharp-eyes."

The lad felt flattered, as if he himself had driven up the mobile shop. He was happy because he'd brought them the news, because he dashed out into the yard together with them, because together with them he stood there at the van's open doors. But the women immediately forgot him. They had more important things to attend to. The assortment of wares lit up their eyes. There were three women in all: old grandma, Aunt Bekai—his mother's sister, the wife of the most important man in the cordon, warden Orozkul—and the wife of handyman Seidakhmat: young Guljamal, with her daughter always in her arms. Three women in all. But they made so much fuss, engaged in so much grabbing, rummaging and scrutinising that the mobile shop man had to ask them to form a queue and stop babbling all at once.

However his words had no great effect on the women. First they grabbed everything in sight, then began to pick out things, and finally to return the rejected items. They put things aside, tried them on, argued, exchanged doubts, and asked the same questions a dozen times. They didn't like this, found that too dear, and the third item was the wrong colour ... The lad stood to one side. He became bored. His expectation of something extraordinary evaporated; the joy he'd felt when he caught sight of the mobile shop on the mountain disappeared too. The mobile shop suddenly turned into an ordinary lorry, crammed with a pile of assorted rubbish.

The vendor frowned: now it was doubtful whether these old hens were going to buy anything at all. What had brought him here, all this long way, through the mountains?

That's the way it turned out. The women began to back away, their ardour cooled, and they even appeared somewhat tired. For some reason, they began to make excuses, either for each other's sake or for the mobile shop man's. Old grandma was the first to complain: she had no money. And no money meant no wares. Aunt Bekai couldn't undertake a large purchase without her husband. Aunt Bekai was the unhappiest woman on earth because she had no children, for which Orozkul beat her in his drunkenness, which brought suffering to grandfather too, for Bekai was his daughter. Aunt Bekai bought a few trifles and two bottles of vodka. Which was in vain: it would only make things worse for her. Old grandma gave in to her disfavour.

"What's the matter with you?" she hissed so that the mobile shop man wouldn't hear. "Begging for disasters to bring down on your own head?"

"I know," Aunt Bekai cut her short.

"You're a fool," said old grandma, whispering even lower, but with a kind of malicious joy. If it weren't for the mobile shop man, she would have upbraided Aunt Bekai. Whew, how they went at each other . . .

Young Guljamal came to the rescue. She launched into an explanation to the vendor of how her Seidakhmat was planning to go to the city soon, and money was needed in the city — which is why she couldn't loosen her purse strings.

So they stood around the mobile shop this way, buying a few things 'for farthings', as the vendor said, and then broke up for home. Can anyone call this business! Spitting in the direction of the departed women, the vendor began to pick up the wares that had been turned inside out, so that he could get behind the wheel and get out. Then he noticed the little boy.

"What's on your mind, big ears?" he asked. The little tyke had protruding ears, a thin neck and a large round head. "You want to buy something? Hurry up, I'm closing. Got any money?"

The vendor asked in passing, just for something to say, but the little boy answered in earnest.

"No sir, I've got no money." He shook his head.

"I bet you do," drawled the vendor with affected mistrust. "You're all money bags around here, you only make out you're broke . . . What's that there in your pocket — money, isn't it?"

"No sir," answered the lad with the same seriousness and sincerity while turning out his threadbare pocket. (His other pocket was sewn tightly closed.)

"That means you've spilled out all your dough, I suppose. Take a look where you were running. You'll find it."

They fell silent.

"Who do you belong to?" the vendor resumed his questioning. "Old Momun, is it?"

The lad nodded in answer.

"You're his grandson, I suppose?"

"Yes," the boy nodded again.

"And where's your mother?"

The boy said nothing. He didn't want to talk about this.

"She doesn't send a word about herself to anybody, your mother? You don't know yourself—is that it?"

"I don't know."

"And your father? Don't know too?"

The boy was silent.

"What's all this, then, my friend? You don't know anything?" the vendor reproached him playfully. "Well, okay, if that's the way it is. Here." He pulled out a handful of candies. "And look after yourself."

The lad backed away in shyness.

"Go on, take them. Don't hold me up. I've got to get moving."

The lad put the candies in his pocket and made ready to run after the lorry—to accompany the mobile shop to the road. He hailed Baltek, a fearfully lazy, shaggy dog. Orozkul was always threatening to shoot him: why keep that kind of mut, he kept saying. But grandfather prevailed on him again and again to wait a bit: the thing to do, he'd propose, was to raise a sheep dog and then take Baltek somewhere and leave him. Baltek couldn't care less about all this: when he was full, he slept; when hungry, he'd keep licking up to the nearest person, strangers as soon as his own masters—quite indiscriminately, as long as someone threw him something. That's the kind of dog Baltek was. But sometimes he'd chase after cars, out of boredom. True, not very far. Only until he'd gained full speed, after which he'd turn around and trot home. An unreliable dog. Still, it was a hundred times better to run with a dog than without one. Whatever he lacked, he was still a dog.

On the sly, so that the vendor wouldn't see, the lad tossed Baltek a piece of candy. "Get set," he warned the dog. "We're going to run a long way." Baltek began to yelp gently and wiggle his tail in the hope of more. But the lad decided against tossing another candy. The man might be insulted: after all, it wasn't for the dog that he'd given a whole handful.

At this very moment, grandfather appeared. The old man had been to the apiary. From the apiary, you couldn't see what was happening behind the houses. But it turned out that grandfather arrived just in time, before the mobile shop drove off. A coincidence. Otherwise, his grandson wouldn't have had a briefcase. The lad was in luck that day.

Old Momun, whom sages nicknamed Efficacious Momun, was known by everyone in the region, and he knew everyone. Momun merited this nickname on the strength of his unfailing amiability to everyone he knew even in the slightest degree and his constant readiness to do anything for anyone, to oblige everyone. However, his zeal was appreciated by no one, just as gold wouldn't be valued if it were suddenly distributed free. No one gave Momun the respect due people his age. He was treated unceremoniously. At great funeral banquets of some renowned elder of the Bugu clan—and Momun was born a Buguan, was very proud of this and would never miss a funeral banquet of one of his clansmen—Momun was often charged with the slaughtering of the cattle, the greeting of the honoured guests and helping with their dismounting. He also helped with the serving of the tea—as well, sometimes, as the splitting of the wood and carrying of the water. Could anyone claim that there was little to attend to at great funerals with all those guests from all parts? Momun did everything he was assigned quickly and easily—and, most important, did not lie down on the job like the others. The young village brides, whose duty it was to welcome and feed this great horde of guests, observed Momun coping with the work and commented about it.

"What would we have done if it weren't for Efficacious Momun?"

And it turned out that the old man, who'd come with his

grandson from far away, would assume the role of a kind of apprentice *dzhigit** samovarboy. Anyone else in his place would have exploded with insult, but Momun was unconcerned.

And no one was surprised that old Efficacious Momun waited on the guests—this is what had made him Efficacious Momun all his life. It was his own fault that he was Efficacious Momun. If one of the newcomers expressed surprise—what are you, an elderly man, doing running women's errands; have the young chaps in this village all gone extinct, for goodness sake? —Momun would answer calmly.

"The dead man was my brother." (He considered all Buguans his brothers. But to no lesser degree, the other guests were also his 'brothers'.) "Who should see to his funeral feast if not I? That's why we Buguans are all in kinship, all descendants from our progenitress herself, Horned Deer-Mother. And she, wonderous Deer-Mother, bequeathed us friendship in life as well as in memory . . ."

That's the kind of man Efficacious Momun was!

Old and young were on 'tu' terms with him and felt free to joke with him—he was a harmless old fellow. No one had to reckon much with him either—he was a meek old fellow. It's not for nothing that they say: people never forgive someone who can't make himself be respected. And he didn't know how.

He could do lots of things in life. At various times, he worked at carpentry, saddle-making and rick-making. In his younger days on a collective farm, he made ricks so well that it was a shame to pull them down in winter. The rain streamed down them like water off a duck's back, and snow lay as smoothly on top of them as on a gabled roof. During the war, he was a labour-soldier building factory walls in Magnitogorsk, and was designated a Stakhanovite. He returned, built log houses in the cordon and became a forester. Although he was officially listed

* *Dzhigit*: a skilled young horseman.

as a handyman, it was he who looked after the forest in fact, and Orozkul, his son-in-law, spent most of his time on eating-and-drinking rounds of his acquaintances. Only when his superiors arrived on a surprise visit would Orozkul himself take them around to inspect the forest and fix up a hunt—in these cases, he played the man in charge ... Momun looked after the cattle and worked in the apiary. All his life, he was busy with work and errands from morning to evening, but he never learned to make people respect him.

Momun's appearance too was far from a chieftain's. He lacked all earmarks of solemnity, importance and sternness. He was a simple good soul, and this unrewarded human virtue was apparent in him from the first glance. In all eras, this kind of person has been admonished: "Don't be good, be hard. That's what you need—to be tough." But to his own misfortune, he remained incorrigibly kindhearted. His face was all smiles and a thousand wrinkles, and his eyes perpetually asked: "What do you need? Do you want me to do something for you? This very minute, just tell me what you need ..."

His nose was soft and duck-like, as if lacking all cartilage. And was shortish as well: a quick-moving old fellow, like an adolescent.

He wore a beard, but even this hadn't worked out. It was nothing more than a source of amusement. Two or three reddish little hairs stuck out on his naked chin—that was the whole of the beard.

It's quite a different thing when you suddenly come upon a man full of weight and years riding along a road, a man with a beard like a sheaf of wheat, wearing an expensive hat and a bulky fur coat with a wide Persian collar; and mounted on a fine horse too, with a silver-trimmed saddle. Such a man lacks nothing to be a sage or prophet, and there's no need to feel small about bowing to his kind. They're esteemed everywhere. But Momun was stuck with having been born only Efficacious

Momun. Perhaps his only advantage lay in not being apprehensive about lowering himself in someone else's eyes. (If he didn't sit in the right place, say the right things, give the right answers, smile the right smiles; wrong, wrong and always out of place . . .) In this sense, Momun, although himself unaware of it, was a man of rare happiness. Many people die not so much from a disease as from an obsession which gnaws incessantly at them: to pass themselves off for more than they are. (Who doesn't want to be known as clever, worthy, handsome – and at the same time formidable, just and decisive? . . .)

But Momun wasn't any of these. He was an odd-ball and people treated him as an odd-ball.

Only one thing could give strong offence to Momun: to forget to invite him to a family council about the arrangements for someone's funeral feast . . . In this case, he was deeply insulted and suffered his slight keenly. Not because he had been ignored, however – he never decided anything at the councils, after all; he merely attended – but because the discharge of an ancient tradition had been violated.

Momun had his misfortunes and sorrows, which brought him suffering and nocturnal tears. Outsiders knew almost nothing about them. But his own people knew well.

When Momun saw his grandson next to the mobile shop, he immediately perceived that the boy had been disappointed by something. Since the vendor was a visitor, however, he first turned to him. He quickly dismounted and offered the vendor both hands.

"*Asalam aleikum*, great trader," he said, half in jest and half seriously. "Has your caravan arrived safely, is your commerce going well?" Ringed in radiance, Momun shook the vendor's hand. "Much water has flowed under the bridge since we've seen each other. Welcome!"

The vendor chuckled condescendingly at his speech and

homely looks—the same old, worn-out tarpaulin boots, sackcloth breeches made by his old woman, shabby little jacket browned with rain and sun and a rough felt hat. Then he answered Momun.

"The caravan's in one piece. Only look what's been going on: a merchant travels all the way to you, and you wander off from the merchant by hill and dale. And order your wives to hold on to their kopeks, like their souls before death. If you'd swamp this place with goods, nobody here would cut a purse string."

"Don't be harsh on us, old chap," Momun apologised embarrassedly. "If we knew you were coming, we wouldn't have gone off. And as for being low on money, what can't be cured must be endured. When we sell our potatoes in the autumn..."

"Talk's cheap," the vendor interrupted. "I know all about you smelly *bais*.* You sit pretty in your mountains with all the land and hay you want. Forest on all sides—it'd take you over three days to drive around it. You raise cattle, yes? Keep bees? And too stingy to part with a kopek. Why don't you buy this here silk blanket. Or there's one sewing machine left..."

"Honest to God, I don't have that kind of money," said Momun, justifying himself.

"You suppose I'll believe that? You're an old skin-flint, you bury your gold. For what?"

"Honest to God no—I swear by Horned Deer-Mother."

"All right then, take some corduroy. You can make yourself a new pair of trousers."

"I'd buy some, I swear by Horned Deer-Mother..."

"Aw, what's the use of talking to you," said the vendor,

---

* *Bai*: an exploiting Asian landlord, with the connotation of a petty rajah. They no longer exist under Soviet rule, and the word is sometimes used as a term of slight contempt.

flapping his hand in disgust. "I should never have come. And where's Orozkul?"

"He pushed off in the morning—to Aksai, probably. He's got some business with the shepherds..."

"Eating and drinking, I suppose," specified the vendor with a knowing look.

An awkward pause descended.

"Please don't take offence, my dear fellow," Momun began again. "In the autumn, God willing, we'll sell our potatoes..."

"Autumn's a long way off."

"Well, if that's the way it's worked out, don't judge us for it. For the love of God, come on in and have some tea."

"That's not what I came for," the vendor refused.

He began to shut the van door, but at that moment glanced at the grandson, who was standing near the old man, already gripping the dog's ear in readiness to chase after the lorry. "Well, at least buy this briefcase," said the vendor. "It must be getting time for the kid here to go to school. How old is he?"

Momun immediately snatched at this idea: he'd have bought at least something from the dogged mobile shop man, and his grandson really did need a briefcase—he'd be starting school the coming autumn.

"You're absolutely right," bustled Momun, "I never thought of that. Of course: he's seven, going on eight... Come over here," he called to his grandson.

Grandfather rummaged in his pockets and fished out a hidden fiver. It had obviously been with him for a considerable time, for it was folded and pressed flat.

"Here you are, big ears." The vendor winked slyly to the lad and presented him with the briefcase. "Now go study. And if you don't get the hang of reading and writing, you'll end up with your grandfather forever in the mountains."

"He'll cope, all right. He's my bright little boy," Momun

answered, counting his change. Then he glanced at his grandson, who was awkwardly holding the brand-new briefcase, and pressed him into his arms. "Good," he said quietly. "You'll go to school in the autumn." Grandfather's tough, weighty palm came down on the lad's head.

The boy felt a tight squeeze in his throat and was acutely aware of his grandfather's leanness and the familiar scent of his clothing. Momun smelled of dry hay and the sweat of a hardworking man. Sure, secure, and terribly dear—perhaps the only person on earth who doted on the boy turned out to be this simple, slightly outlandish old man whom clever types called Efficacious Momun . . . And what of it? Whatever he was, it was good to have him as a grandfather.

The lad himself hadn't suspected that his happiness would be so great. Until now, he hadn't thought of school. So far, he'd only seen children going to school—over there, on the other side of the mountains, in the villages along the Issik-Kul, where he and grandfather went to funeral feasts of renowned Buguan elders.

But from this moment, the lad never parted with his briefcase. Exulting and swaggering, he dashed off immediately to make the rounds of all the cordon's inhabitants. At first he showed his prize to old grandma—as if to say that his grandfather had bought him this—and then to Aunt Bekai. She too was impressed by the briefcase and praised the lad himself.

Aunt Bekai was rarely in a pleasant mood. Gloomy and irritated, she usually took no notice of her nephew. She was too preoccupied with other matters. Her own troubles weighed on her. Old grandma said that if she had children, she'd be a completely different woman. And Orozkul, her husband, would also be a different person. Then grandfather Momun would also be a different person, instead of the kind he was. Although he had two daughters—Aunt Bekai as well as the lad's mother, her younger sister—things were unhappy all the same: it's bad when you're childless and still worse when your children are childless. That's what old grandma said. How to understand her? . . .

After Aunt Bekai, the lad ran off to show the purchase to young Guljamal and her little girl. From there he went down to Seidakhmat, who was mowing the hay. Again he ran past the ginger 'camel' rock and again had no time to pat him on the hump. He passed 'saddle', 'wolf' and 'tank', then ran farther, keeping to the river bank. The trail cut through thorny bushes; then he followed a long windrow of hay on the meadow and at last reached Seidakhmat.

Seidakhmat was alone there today. Grandfather had mowed his own plot long before, together with Orozkul's. They'd already carted away the hay. Old grandma and Aunt Bekai had raked it up, Momun pitchforked it together, and the lad helped grandfather lay the hay on the wagon. They built two ricks near the cowshed. Grandfather constructed them so carefully that no manner of rain would leak in. Ricks as smooth as if they'd been combed.

The same pattern was followed every year. Orozkul never mowed, but left everything to his father-in-law: Orozkul was the boss, after all. "If I have a mind to," he'd say, "I'll fire you all at one stroke." This was directed to grandfather and Seidakhmat. And pronounced when he was pickled. But he could never chase grandfather away: if he did, who'd do the work? Just try to make a go without grandfather. There was much to see to in the forest, especially in autumn. Grandfather always said: "The forest's not a flock of sheep, it won't scatter or stray. But it takes no less looking after. When there's a fire or a flash flood strikes from the mountain, a tree doesn't jump aside. It won't move from its place, but is destroyed right where it stands. That's what foresters are for: so that the trees won't be lost." And Orozkul wouldn't chase off Seidakhmat because Seidakhmat was gentle. He didn't interfere in anyone else's business and didn't argue. But although gentle and sturdy, he was also lazy and liked to sleep. That's why he settled on forestry. Grandfather said that on the state farm, fellows like him raced lorries or took on the ploughing with their tractors. But in his private vegetable patch, Seidakhmat's potatoes were overgrown with weed. Guljamal finally had to take over the garden herself, working with her child in her arms.

Seidakhmat also put off starting the haying. Even grandfather had scolded him the day before yesterday. "Last winter," he said, "it wasn't you I felt sorry for, but the animals. That's why I gave you some of my hay. If you're counting on this old fogey's hay again, tell me straight out and I'll do the mowing for you." Seidakhmat took the hint and began swinging his scythe that morning.

Hearing quick steps behind his back, Seidakhmat spun around, wiping his face with his shirt-sleeve.

"What do you want? Did somebody call me or something?"

"No. I've got a briefcase. Here it is. Grandfather bought it. I'm going to school."

"You ran all the way down here for that?" Seidakhmat produced a boisterous laugh. "Grandfather Momun's like that" – he twisted his finger at his temple – "and you're heading the same way. All right, let's see your briefcase." He clicked the catch, twirled the briefcase in his hand and returned it, mockingly shaking his head. "Wait a minute!" he exclaimed. "What school are you going to? Where is it, this school of yours?"

"What do you mean, what school? The farm school."

"You're going to walk to Jelesai?" marvelled Seidakhmat. "But that's across the mountains, not less than five kilometres."

"Grandfather said he's going to take me there on his horse."

"Back and forth every day? The old man's full of poppycock. It's about time for him to go to school himself. He can share your desk with you, and when classes are over—back home together!" Seidakhmat split his sides with laughter. He thought it extremely funny to picture grandfather Momun sitting at the same school desk with his grandson.

The lad maintained a puzzled silence.

"Oh, I only said that for laughs," explained Seidakhmat.

He gave the lad a tweak on the nose and pulled the peak of his hat—grandfather's hat—over the boy's eyes. Momun never wore the Forestry Department's uniform cap; he was ashamed of it. ("What am I, some kind of boss? I wouldn't trade my own Kirghiz hat for any in the world.") In summer, therefore, an antediluvian hat of thick felt rode Momun's head, a 'former' *ak-kulpak**—a round white cap edged with worn black sateen around the brim; and in winter, an ancient sheepskin skullcap, also ragged. He had given his green uniform cap of the Forestry Service to his grandson to wear.

The lad was unhappy that Seidakhmat had received his news so scoffingly. He raised the peak of his cap to his forehead sullenly, and when Seidakhmat reached out to tweak his nose again, jerked his head back and snapped:

"Leave me alone!"

"My my—what an angry one you are," grinned Seidakhmat. "But don't take it to heart. Your briefcase fits the bill." He patted the boy on the shoulder. "Now shove off. I've still got to mow all day ..."

Spitting on his palms, Seidakhmat retrieved the scythe.

The lad ran home, again along the same trail and once more at full speed past the same rocks. For the time being, he had no time to play around with rocks. A briefcase was a serious matter.

The lad liked to hold conversations with himself. But this time he spoke not to himself but the briefcase: "Don't you believe him, my grandfather's nothing like that. He's not a

* *Ak-kulpak*: a national Kirghizian cap of white felt in Central Asian style.

bit cunning, that's why people laugh at him. Because he's not the tiniest bit cunning. He's going to take you and me to school. You don't know where school is yet? It's not so far. I'll show you. We'll take a look at it through the binoculars from Guard Mountain. And I'll show you my white steamship too. Only first we'll duck into the shed. That's where my binoculars are hidden. I'm supposed to look after the calf, but I always go off to look at the white steamship. The calf's grown up already—he pulls you around so, you can't control him. Still and all, he's picked up the habit of sucking milk from a cow. But the cow's his mother and doesn't grudge the milk. Understand? Mothers never grudge anything. That's what Guljamal says, and she has her own little girl . . . Soon they'll start milking the cow and then we'll put the calf out to pasture. Then we'll climb up on Guard Mountain and look at the white steamship. You know, I talk with the binoculars like this too. Now there'll be three of us—me, you and the binoculars . . ."

In this fashion, he returned home. He very much enjoyed talking with the briefcase. He was about to continue the conversation, telling things about himself that the briefcase didn't yet know. But he was interrupted. From off to the side came the clatter of a horse's hoofs. Then, from behind the trees, a horseman appeared on a grey horse. It was Orozkul. He was also returning home. On the grey horse Alabash, whom he allowed no one but himself to ride, all saddled up in his parade gear, with brass stirrups, breast straps and tinkling silver pendants.

Orozkul's hat was cocked on the back of his head, revealing a narrow, reddish forehead. Drowsiness gripped him in the heat. He slept despite the horse's motion. A velveteen tunic, rather unskilfully sewn on the pattern of those worn by the regional authorities, was unbuttoned from top to bottom. His white shirt had pulled out of his belt in front. He was gorged and drunk. A short time before, he had been a guest at someone's table, glutting himself on mare's milk and meat.

When they came to the mountains for summer pasturing, the neighbouring shepherds and horseherders often pressed Orozkul to let them play host to him. But their invitations had a purpose. They needed Orozkul, especially those who were building houses. They had to remain in the mountains, couldn't leave and abandon their herds — and where could they get their hands on building materials, especially timber? But if you got on the good side of Orozkul, it was as simple as that: you had your choice of two or three logs from the forest preserve, and you hauled them away. And if not, you'd wander around the mountains forever with your herd, and your house would take forever to build.

Dozing in the saddle, stuffed and important, Orozkul rode on, lackadaisically resting the toes of his box-calf boots in the stirrups. He nearly flew out of the saddle when the lad ran up to meet him, waving the briefcase.

"Uncle Orozkul, I've got a briefcase. I'm going to school. Look, I've got a briefcase."

"Why don't you go to . . ." swore Orozkul, yanking on the reins in fright.

He peered at the lad with bloodshot, half-awake eyes, puffed up with drink.

"What are you doing here?"

"I'm going home. I've got a briefcase, I was just showing it to Seidakhmat," said the lad in a sinking voice.

"Yeah yeah — go play," barked Orozkul, and rode on, rolling unsteadily in the saddle. What did he care about a stupid briefcase, about his wife's nephew, a kid abandoned by his parents, when he himself had been so abused by fate? When God wouldn't give him his own son, a boy of his own blood, while others got all the children they wanted, without limit?

Orozkul began to sniffle, then uttered a sob. He was choked with self-pity and resentment. He felt terribly sorry for himself — sorry that his life would pass without leaving a trace on earth. A wave of anger towards his barren wife swept over him. It was all her fault, that damned woman who had gone empty all these years...

"I'll show you!" Orozkul threatened to himself, clenching his beefy fists and producing a suppressed groan to stop himself from crying aloud. He already knew that he would beat her when he came home. It happened every time Orozkul drank: sorrow and bitterness made this bull-like man take leave of his senses.

The lad followed behind him on the trail and was surprised when Orozkul suddenly disappeared. Turning towards the river, Orozkul dismounted, dropped the reins and pushed his way through the tall grass. Bent over and staggering, he pressed his hands full against his face and pulled his head into his shoulders. At the bank, Orozkul squatted and splashed his face with handfuls of water from the river.

"His head's probably hurting him because of the heat," the lad decided when he saw what Orozkul was up to. He didn't know that Orozkul was crying and, try as he did, couldn't control his sobs. He cried because it wasn't his son who had rushed out to meet him, and because he knew something in himself was lacking. Something that would have allowed him to say at least a few human words to that boy with the briefcase.

II

From the summit of Guard Mountain, the view was open on all sides. Lying on his stomach, the lad fitted the binoculars to his eyes. They were powerful field binoculars which had been awarded to grandad long long ago in recognition of his lengthy service in the cordon. The old man disliked fussing with binoculars: "My own two eyes are no worse." On the other hand, his grandson had fallen in love with them.

This time he had climbed the mountain with the binoculars and the briefcase.

At first objects fluttered about, shifting in the round lenses; then, suddenly, clarity and immobility were established. That was the most fascinating moment of all. The lad held his breath so as not to disturb his focus and drank in the scene as if he himself had created it. Then he shifted his gaze to another point and again everything was dislocated and out of focus. The lad set to work adjusting the oculars.

From here, everything was visible in all directions. Including the very highest snow-covered summits, than which only the sky was higher. They rose up behind all the mountains;

atop all the mountains and above the whole earth. And the mountains lower than the snowy giants — the thickly forested ones, covered down below with leafy thickets and above with stands of dark pine. And the mountains of Kungei, which rose up towards the sun; on the Kungei slopes, nothing grew but grass. And the still smaller mountains towards the lake, which were no more than naked, rocky knolls left after landslides. The knolls descended into the valley, and the valley narrowed directly down into the lake. On the same side lay fields, orchards and settlements . . . Yellow zigzags already showed through the green of the sown areas: harvest time was approaching. Tiny lorries crept along the roads like mice, followed by long trails of whirling dust. At the farthest corner of the earth, as far as you could see, beyond the sandy strip of shore was the deep blue of the lake's convex curvature. This was the Issik-Kul. Water and sky joined together there. Beyond that, there was nothing. The lake was immobile, dazzling and vacant. Only near the bank stirred the barely-visible white foam of the surf.

The lad gazed in this direction for a long time. "The white steamship hasn't come yet," he said to the briefcase. "Let's you and I have another look at our school."

From here, the entire neighbouring valley beyond the mountain was visible. Through the binoculars, you could even make out the yarn in the hands of the old women who were sitting outside their houses, under the windows.

The Jelesai Valley was bare of forest; only a few lonely old pine trees remained here and there after its cutting long ago. Once there had been a forest here. Now there were rows of cattle pens under slate roofs, and you could see big black piles of manure and straw. Young pedigree animals for the dairy were raised there. And there too, not far from the cattle pens, a stunted little street found room for itself — the cattle breeders' settlement. The little street ran down from a small hillock. At the very edge of the street, its far end, stood a little house with an uninhabited appearance. This was the four-year primary school. The pupils in older classes went off to study in a boarding school on the state farm. But the little children went to this one.

The lad had visited the settlement with grandfather to go to the village medical assistant when he'd had a sore throat. Now, through the binoculars, he examined the little school intensely under its brownish tiles, with its single ramshackle chimney and its hand-painted sign on a plywood rectangle: 'Mektep'. He couldn't read, but guessed that this was the word that was written. Through the binoculars, everything was visible in the tiniest, unbelievably fine detail. Words of some kind scratched into the mortar walls, a glued-together pane in one of the window frames, the stooped, pock-marked panels of the veranda. He pictured how he would come here with his briefcase and march through that door, on which a large padlock now hung. But what was there, what would happen there, behind that door?

Completing his examination of the school, the lad again directed the binoculars to the lake. But nothing had changed there. The white steamship still hadn't appeared. The lad turned around, settled with his back to the lake and, putting aside the binoculars, began to look downward, below the mountain. Below, directly under the mountain, along the bottom of the elongated hollow, ran the silvery, violent river with its dozens of rapids. Following its bank, the road twisted with the river – then, together with the river, hid itself behind a veer in the gorge. The opposite bank was steep and forested. This was the beginning of the San-Tash forest preserve, rising high up into the mountains until it reached the snow itself. The pine trees grew higher than any others. Amidst the rocks and snow, they stuck up like black brushes on the crests of the mountain chains.

The lad mockingly surveyed the houses, sheds and outhouses in the yards of the cordon. They seemed tiny and fragile from above. Beyond the cordon, farther down the bank, he picked out his own, familiar rocks. He had first distinguished all of them—'camel', 'wolf', 'saddle', 'tank'—from this spot on Guard Mountain through the binoculars. That was when he gave them their names.

The lad smiled mischievously, stood and flung a stone in the direction of his house. But the stone landed right there, just a little way down the mountain. The lad sat down again in the same place and began surveying the cordon through the binoculars. First through the large lenses into the smaller ones—the houses flew away far into the distance, and turned into little toy boxes. The boulders became pebbles. And grandfather's pond in the shallow of the river seemed even funnier—a drop in the bucket. The lad grinned, shook his head, and quickly shifting the binoculars right way round, adjusted the oculars. His cherished boulders, enlarged to huge proportions, seemed to be resting their foreheads against the lenses. 'Camel', 'wolf', 'saddle' and 'tank' were extremely impressive: they had notches, cracks and spots of rusty lichen on their sides—and most important, they really looked very much like what the lad saw in them. "Gee, what a wolf! And the tank—he's really something . . ."

Beyond the rocks lay grandfather's pond in the shallow. You could see this part of the bank very clearly through the binoculars. Here the water streamed over the wide, pebbly shallows from the rapids, and surging up over the shoals, ran back into the main stream. The water in the shallow came up to the knees, but the current was so strong that it could easily wash a boy like him straight into the river. So as not to be carried off by the current, the lad would hold on to a rose willow on the bank—the bush grew on the very edge of the bank, with some of its branches on dry land and others wriggling in the river—and dipped into the water. What kind of swimming do you call that? Like a horse on a tether. And how many other troubles there were—how he was scolded and cursed! Old grandma would lecture grandfather: "If he's washed away, he can take all the blame on himself, I'm not going to lift a finger. Who needs him anyway? His own mother and father abandoned him. And I've got worries enough of my own, I've come to the end of my strength."

What could you say to her? The old woman was right in a way. Still, it was a pity for the boy not to swim: after all, the river was right there, almost at his door. No matter how the old woman tried to fill him with fear, the boy kept ducking into the water all the same. That was when Momun finally decided to build a pond out of rocks on the sand bank, so that the little tyke would have a safe place to swim.

How many rocks old man Momun shifted to the river, having picked out the larger ones so that the current wouldn't roll them away. He carried the rocks over by pressing them against his stomach; then, standing in the water, he laid one upon another with the calculation that the water should flow freely between the rocks on one side, and escape just as freely on the other. Funny-looking, skinny, with his scraggy little beard, he worked fastidiously a whole day over the pond, in wet trousers clinging to his body. In the evening, he lay flat on his back, coughed, and found himself unable to straighten the small of his back. At this point, old grandma yielded wholly to her scorn.

"The little one's a fool—but he's only little. What can you say about an old fool? Why the devil did you knock yourself up that way? You feed him, clothe him—what else does he need? You hippety-hop to his every little whim. Ekh, nothing good will come of it . . ."

Despite all this, the pond on the shallow turned out very well indeed. Now the lad bathed without fear. Holding on to the branch, he climbed down from the bank and plunged into the stream. Invariably with his eyes open. Open eyes because fish in water swim with them open. That was his curious daydream: he wanted to turn into a fish. And to swim away.

Gazing now at the pond through the binoculars, the lad pictured how he would rip off his shirt and trousers and, naked and huddled up, slip into the water. The water in mountain rivers is always very cold; it takes your breath away. But then you get used to it. He pictured how, holding on to a branch of the rose willow, he always plunged face first into the stream. How the water would gurgle up over his head noisily, and the tingling scurry up his stomach, back and legs. Underwater, the noises of the outside world died away, leaving only a babbling in his ears. Goggling zealously, he would examine everything visible underwater. His eyes would smart. He'd feel a stinging in his eyes. But he'd smile to himself haughtily and even stick out his tongue in the water. That would be for old grandma. Let her learn that he'd never drown and didn't fear a thing. Then he'd let go of the branch and the water would carry him away, pull him downstream until he could plant his feet on the rocks around the pond. At this point, his breath would give out. He'd jump out of the water in a single leap, climb up on the bank and dash over to the rose willow bush again. And keep at this over and over. He was ready to swim a hundred times a day in grandfather's pond. Until he finally turned into a fish. No matter how, he had to turn into a fish, he absolutely *must* . . .

Having scrutinised the river bank, the lad shifted the binoculars to his own yard. Chickens, turkeys and turkey-poults, an axe leaning against a block, a smoking samovar and all kinds of stuff cluttered around the house—all these things became so unbelievably big and seemed so close that the lad involuntarily reached out his hand to them. At this moment, to his great horror, he saw a brownish calf in the binoculars, enlarged to elephantine proportions. He was peacefully chewing at the laundry hung out on a line. The calf's eyes were screwed up with pleasure and saliva dripped from its muzzle—how wonderful it was to munch a whole mouthful of old grandma's dress.

"Hey you—you idiot!" The lad jumped up with the binoculars and began to wave his hand. "Get out of there this minute, do you hear? Move yourself—clear off! Baltek, *Baltek!*" (Framed in the lenses, the dog was stretched out alongside the house, dead to the world.) "Go for him, get at him," he commanded the dog in despair. But Baltek did not so much as prick an ear. He lay in the shade as if nothing was happening and nothing ever would.

At this moment, old grandma emerged from the house. When she saw the disaster, the old woman threw up her hands. Then grabbed a broom and fell upon the calf. The calf ran away, with old grandma in hot pursuit. Not losing her for an instant in the binoculars, the lad squatted down again so as not to be seen on the mountain. Having driven off the calf, the old woman made her way back towards the house, cursing and panting from exertion and anger. The lad saw her as if he were right there at her side—even closer. He held a close-up on her in his lenses, as in the cinema when the whole screen is somebody's face. He saw her yellowed eyes, now narrowed in fury. He watched her whole face, wrinkled into deep creases, going a deep red. As in the cinema when the sound suddenly goes off, old grandma's lips twitched in quick and soundless motion, revealing her chipped teeth, few and far between.

From afar, you couldn't make out what the old woman was shouting, but the boy felt her words so distinctly and precisely that she might have been speaking right into his ear. Zounds, how she was cursing him! He knew it all by heart: "All right, just you wait. You'll come back. I'll show you. And I won't pay any attention to grandfather. How many times have I said it: those fool look-glasses should be tossed out once and for all. He's sneaked off to the mountain—yes, again. I hope it drops to hell, that damn steamship. I hope it burns down, I hope it sinks..."

The boy on the mountain sighed deeply. Just on the day when his briefcase was bought, when he was already dreaming about how he'd go to school, it had to go and happen that he'd forget the calf...

The old woman did not regain her composure. Maintaining a steady stream of cursing, she examined her chewed-up dress. With her daughter in her arms, Guljamal went out to give her comfort and calm her down. But in the process of complaining to her, old grandma succumbed even more to her rage. She shook her fists in the direction of the mountain. Her dark bony fists loomed up threateningly in the lenses. "He's cooked up a fine way to play for himself. I hope it drops to hell, that damn steamship. I hope it burns down, I hope it sinks..."

The samovar in the yard was already boiling. Through the binoculars, you could see a jet of steam escaping from under the lid. Aunt Bekai came out to attend to it. Which started everything all over again. Old grandma shoved the munched-up dress almost into her nose as if to say, here, take a good look at your nephew's tricks.

Aunt Bekai began to reason with her in an attempt to soothe her anger. The lad guessed what she was saying: just about what she always did. "Calm yourself, *Eneke*.* He's still young, just a silly little kid—you can't expect much from him. He's alone here, he has no friends. Why shout, what's the use of building fear in the boy?"

To which old grandma doubtlessly replied: "Don't you tell me how to behave. Try to bear some children of your own

* *Eneke*: the Kirghiz equivalent of the Russian *matushka*: roughly 'dear, sweet, respected, old mother'.

and then you'll know what to expect from them. What's he hanging around there on the mountain for? Too busy with his nonsense to tie up the calf. What's he up there spying at? Looking out for his good-for-nothing parents? The ones who scattered to the winds the minute they gave birth to him? It's easy for you to talk, you barren thing..."

Even at that distance, the lad saw Aunt Bekai's sunken cheeks turn a deathly pale through the binoculars. He watched her whole body begin to throb and — he knew exactly how his aunt would pay her back — saw her blurt fierce words into her step-mother's face.

"What about you, you old witch — how many sons did *you* raise — or daughters? Who the hell do you think you are?"

And oh, what now began. Old grandma howled in outrage. Guljamal tried to reconcile the women; she talked soothingly to them, hugged old grandma and tried to lead her back into her house. But the latter became more and more incensed, scuttling around the yard as if mad. Aunt Bekai seized the samovar and fairly ran back home with it, spilling some of the boiling water. Old grandma sunk wearily onto the chopping block, sobbing and bitterly bemoaning her fate. Now the lad was forgotten; the culprits were none other than the Lord God himself and the whole wide world.

"You mean *me*? You asked me who *I* am?" screamed old grandma at her departed step-daughter. "If God hadn't punished me, if he hadn't taken my five babies, if my son, my one and only, didn't meet a bullet during the war at eighteen, if my dear, darling man Taigara hadn't frozen to death with a flock of sheep in a terrible snowstorm — do you really think I'd be here, among you forest types? Do you really think I'm anything like you, you dead-wombed creature? Do you really think I'd live out my old age with your father, that imbecile Momun? Cursed God, what faults and sins did you punish me for?"

The lad removed the binoculars from his eyes and sadly hung his head. "How can we go home now?" he said softly to the briefcase. "All this happened because of me and that idiot calf. And because of you too, binoculars. You're always inviting me to look at the white steamship. You're guilty too."

The lad looked around in all directions. Everywhere were mountains, cliffs, rocks and forests. Glittering streams flew down silently from glaciers above. Only here, down below, did the water seem to acquire a voice — to produce its incessant, eternal sounds in the river. The mountains were vast and limitless. At this moment, the boy felt very small, entirely alone and wholly lost. Alone with the mountains, everywhere the great mountains.

The sun was already starting its descent towards the lake. The heat was becoming less powerful. The first short shadows were appearing on the eastern slopes. Now the sun would sink lower and lower, and the shadows would creep down to the foot of the mountains. At this time of day, the white steamship usually appeared on the Issik-Kul.

The lad directed the binoculars to the farthest visible point and held his breath. There it was! Everything was immediately forgotten: there, in the distance, on the bluest of blue edge of the Issik-Kul, the white steamship appeared. It was underway. There it was! Long, powerful and beautiful, with its funnels all in a row. It travelled straight and smooth, as if on a string. The lad hurriedly wiped the lenses with his shirt-tail and again adjusted the oculars. The ship's outlines became even clearer. Now you could see it rolling gently on the waves, and how its stern left a light trail of foam. Motionless, the lad watched the white steamship in rapture. Had it been in his power, he would have begged the white steamship to come closer, so that he could see the people on board. But the steamship knew nothing of this. It moved along its own course slowly and majestically, from an unknown origin to an unknown destination.

For a long time, the ship could be seen steaming on; for a long time, the lad thought about how he'd turn into a fish and swim down the river to join it, the white steamship.

When he first saw the white steamship one day on Guard Mountain, saw it there on the blue Issik-Kul, his heart chimed so from its dazzling beauty that he decided at once. His father — an Issik-Kul sailor — had to work precisely there, on the white steamship. And the lad believed this, because he very much wanted to.

He remembered neither his father nor his mother. He'd never seen them, even once. Neither of them visited him even a single time. But the lad knew: his father was a sailor on the Issik-Kul and his mother, after the divorce from his father, had left her son with his grandfather and moved to the city. She moved — meaning vanished. Moved to a distant city beyond the mountains, the lake, and yet more mountains.

Grandfather Momun once went to that city to sell potatoes. He stayed there, seeing to the selling, a whole week and when he returned, told Aunt Bekai and old grandma over tea that he had seen his daughter — that is, his, the lad's, mother. She worked as a weaver in a big factory of some sort. She had a new family: two daughters whom she put in a municipal kindergarten and saw only once a week. She lived in a large block of flats but in one tiny room, so tiny that you could hardly turn around in it. And no one knew anyone else in the yard — just like at the market. They all lived like that there: they'd come home and lock their doors straightaway. They were always under lock and key, like in jail. And her husband, who seemed to be a driver, carted people around streets in a bus. He left at four o'clock in the morning and came back late in the evening — also hard work. His daughter, Momun related, had cried a lot and begged forgiveness. They were on the list for a new flat, but didn't know when they'd get one. But when they did, she'd take her sonny-boy back with her, if her husband was willing. Meanwhile, she asked the old man to carry on with the present arrangements. Grandfather Momun told her not to grieve. The most important thing was that she live in peace with her husband; everything else would take care of itself. As for her son, she mustn't give in to heartbreak.

"As long as I'm alive, I'll never give the little fellow to anybody. And when I die, God will be his guide. As long as he lives and breathes, he'll work out his own fate . . ." Listening to the old man, Aunt Bekai and old grandma sighed from time to time and even shed tears together.

It was at this very occasion, over tea, that the conversation turned to his father as well. Grandfather had heard that his former son-in-law, the lad's father, was apparently still a sailor serving on the same ship, and that he too had a new family, including two or perhaps three children. They lived near the pier. It was said that he'd given up drinking. And that his new wife always went out with the kids to meet him on the pier. "They must be meeting *his* steamship," the lad thought. "That very one . . ."

The steamship pushed on, slowly moving away. White and long, it glided along the lake's blue glassiness with its funnels smoking — and didn't know that towards it was swimming a lad who'd turned into a fish-boy.

He dreamed of turning into a fish so that everything on him would be fish-like: body, tail, fins and scales — only his head would stay his own. A big round head on a thin neck, with protruding ears and a nose covered with scratches. And the same eyes that he'd had before — not exactly the same, of course, because they'd be able to see like a fish's.

The lad's eyelashes were very long, like the calf's, and something was always making them flutter on their own accord. Guljamal said that if her daughter had his, she'd be a dazzling beauty. But why be beautiful? Or handsome? As if that were any good. For him personally, pretty eyes weren't worth anything; he needed the kind that could see under water.

The transformation would take place in grandfather's pond. One two *three* — and he'd be a fish. Then he'd vault straightaway from the pond into the river, directly into the seething stream, to swim downriver with the current. Then it would go like this: he'd keep leaping up and looking around — because it's dull, after all, to swim only under water. He'd swim fast down the swift river, alongside the red clay precipices, across the rapids, and through the surf, past the mountains and forests. He'd say farewell to his dear boulders. "Goodbye 'lying camel', goodbye 'wolf', goodbye 'saddle', goodbye 'tank'." And when he'd swim past the cordon, he'd leap out of the water and wave his fin to grandfather. "Goodbye *Ata*.* I'll be back soon."

Grandfather would be struck dumb with the wonder of it all and wouldn't know what to do. And old grandma, Aunt Bekai and Guljamal with her daughter — they'd all stand there with their mouths open. Who's ever heard of such a thing? — a person's head on a fish's body. He'd wave his fin to them too: "Goodbye, I'm swimming out to the Issik-Kul and the white steamship. I've got my sailor-papa out there."

Baltek would no doubt jump up to chase along the bank. After all, the dog had never never seen anything like this. But if Baltek got up the courage to jump into the water after him, he'd shout. "No Baltek, no. You mustn't — you'll drown!" All this time, he himself would be swimming on, farther downriver. He'd dive through the ropes of the suspension bridge and keep going farther, past the bushes and wooded parts on the bank. And then, plunging through the roaring gorge, he'd swim right out into the Issik-Kul.

* *Ata:* a Central Asian term for grandfather, indicating high respect and affection.

The Issik-Kul was a whole sea. He'd swim along its waves, from wave to wave, wave to wave, until he'd finally ease right up to the white steamship. "Hello, white steamship, it's me," he'd say to the ship. "I'm the one who was always looking at you through the binoculars." The people on board would be amazed and flock together on the run to examine the wonder. Then he'd say to his father, the sailor: "Hello, papa, I'm your son. I've swum out to you."

"What do you mean, you're my son? Why, you're half-fish and half-human."

"You just take me up there with you, on the ship—and I'll become your real-live natural son."

"Bless my heart! Well then, let's give it a try." And father would lower a net, fish him out of the water and bring him up on deck. Then he'd turn back into himself again. And after this, after this . . .

After this, the white steamship would keep sailing on. The boy would tell his father about everything he knew, about his whole life. About the mountains among which he lived, about his same favourite rocks, about the river and the forest preserve. And about grandfather's pond, where he'd learned to swim like a fish—with his eyes open.

He'd tell, of course, about how his life went with grandfather. His father mustn't think that if the man was called Efficacious Momun, that meant he was bad. There wasn't a single grandfather like him anywhere, he was the very best grandaddy. But he wasn't a bit cunning, that's why everybody laughed at him. Because he wasn't the tiniest bit cunning. But Uncle Orozkul—he shouted at him, screamed at an elderly man! He sometimes even raised his voice at him in front of other people. And instead of standing up for himself, grandfather always forgave Uncle Orozkul—even did his work for him in the forest, the chores and managing things. But work was nothing compared to the rest. When Uncle Orozkul came back drunk, instead of spitting into his wicked eyes, grandfather ran up to greet him, lifted him down from his horse and helped him into his house. He stretched him out on his bed and covered him up with his winter sheepskin so that he wouldn't get a chill or a headache. And afterwards he unsaddled the horse and groomed it, then gave it some fodder. And all because Aunt Bekai's unfertile. Why is it like that, papa? It'd be better like this: if you want children, go ahead and have them; if not, you don't have to.

Grandfather feels bad when Uncle Orozkul beats Aunt Bekai. It'd be easier for him if he beat grandfather himself. How he feels the hurt when Aunt Bekai screams! But what can he do? He wants to rush to his daughter's rescue, but old grandma won't let him. "Keep your nose out of it," she says. "They'll settle it themselves. What business is it of yours, you old geezer? She's not your wife, so sit down and shut up."

"But she's my daughter."

"And what would you do," old grandma answers, "if you didn't live close by, didn't live right next door, but someplace far away? Gallop over to separate them every time? Then who'd keep your daughter for a wife?"

Old grandma who I'm telling you about—she's not the same one as before. You probably don't know her, papa. It's a new grandma. My own granny died when I was small. Then this one came. We have tricky weather sometimes—it can be clear, then cloudy; it can rain and even hail. And old grandma's like that too—you can never tell with her. She can be kind or mean, and sometimes she's neither one nor the other. When she's angry, she wears you right out. Grandfather and I don't say anything. She says that no matter how much you feed or clothe an outsider, you can't expect any good from him. But honest, papa—I'm not an outsider here. I always lived with grandfather. She's the outsider—she came only later. And began to call me an outsider.

In winter, we have snows that come right up to my chin. Gosh, the drifts that pile up! In the forest, you can move about only on Alabash, the grey horse: he ploughs through drifts with his chest. And the wind's so strong you can hardly keep your feet. When the waves whip up on the lake, when your ship rolls from side to side—you should know that it's our San-Tash wind that's rocking the lake. Grandfather told me that long, long ago, enemy forces came here to capture control of our lands. And at that time, such a wind blew up from our San-Tash that the enemy couldn't stay in their saddles. They got off their horses but couldn't even move forward on foot. The wind whipped their faces until they bled. Then they turned away from the wind, but it drove at their backs so that they couldn't look around. It didn't even let them hold their ground, and the wind drove every last one of them from the Issik-Kul. That's the way it was. And now we live with this wind! It starts its blowing right where we are. All winter the forest on the other side of the river creaks, howls and groans in the wind. It's even scary sometimes.

There's an awful lot of work in the forest in winter. Where we are, there are no people at all in winter—not like in summer, when the nomad breeders come. I love it in summer when people with flocks and herds stay overnight on the big meadow. True, they go off into the mountains in the morning, but all the same it's good to be with them. Their women and kids come along in lorries. The lorries transport the *yurts** and all kinds of things they need. After they've settled down a bit, grandfather and I go down to greet them. We greet each and every one with handshakes—me too.

Grandfather says that younger people should always be first to offer their hands to older people. Anyone who doesn't put out his hand doesn't respect people. And besides, grandfather says, out of every seven people, one can turn out to be a

---

* *Yurt:* a circular tent of wood and felt used by the peoples of Central Asia.

prophet. A prophet is a very kind and wise man. Anyone who shakes hands with one will stay happy his whole life. And I say if that's true, why doesn't this prophet say he's a prophet so that we'd all shake his hand? Grandfather laughs. That's the whole point, he says: a prophet doesn't know himself that he's a prophet—he's just an ordinary man. Only a thief knows about himself that he's a thief. I don't quite understand this, but I always greet people, even though I'm sometimes a little ashamed.

But when grandfather and I go down to the meadow, then I'm not embarrassed.

"Welcome to the summering place of your fathers and ancestors. Your cattle and souls are, I trust, in a state of well-being? And your children?" That's the way grandfather talks. But I only shake hands. Everybody knows grandfather and he knows everybody. That makes him feel good. He holds conversations with people, asks them about everything and tells them all about how we live. I don't know what to talk about with the kids. But then we begin playing hide-and-seek and war games—we start having so much fun that I don't want to leave. If only it was always summer, if only I could always play with the other boys on the meadow!

While we're playing, the camp fires begin to burn. I guess you think, papa, that the fires light up the whole meadow. Far from it! It's only bright near the flames, but beyond the little patch of light, it's darker than ever. We play war games in the darkness—hiding or attacking—and it's just as if we were in a real film. If you're the commander, everybody obeys you. It must be fine for a commander to be a commander . . .

Then the moon comes out over the mountains. It's even better in moonlight, but grandfather calls me back in. We go home across the meadow and bushes. The sheep are lying quietly and the horses are grazing all around. We walk home and hear: somebody starts singing a song. A young shepherd probably, or maybe an old one. Grandfather stops me. "Listen. You can't always hear those songs." We stand still and listen. Grandfather sighs. The song makes him nod his head.

Grandfather says that long ago one khan had another khan prisoner. And this khan said to the captive-khan: "If you want to, you can live as my slave. Otherwise I'll fulfil your most cherished wish and then kill you." The other one thought before answering: "I do not wish to live as a slave. I'd rather you kill me, but before this, summon the first shepherd you meet from my homeland." "Why do you want him?" "Before my death, I want to hear him sing." Grandfather says that people give their lives for their native songs. Who are these people? I'd like to see them. I guess they live in big cities?

"Listen—how wonderful to listen," grandfather whispers. "What songs they used to sing, my boy ..." I don't know why, but I begin to feel so sorry for my grandfather and I love him so much that I want to cry.

Early in the morning, everybody's already disappeared from the meadow. They've driven the sheep and horses farther on, into the mountains for the whole summer. Right on their heels, new nomads come, from other collective farms. During the day, they don't stop but go straight on past. But at night, they stay over on the meadow. And grandfather and I go down to greet them. He loves to greet people very much, and I learned how from him. Maybe some day on the meadow I'll shake hands with a real prophet...

In winter, Uncle Orozkul and Aunt Bekai go off to the city to see a doctor. They say that a doctor can help by giving the kinds of medicines that will make a child come. But old grandma always says that it's best of all to go to a holy place. It's somewhere over there beyond the mountains, where cotton grows in the fields. You see, papa, on this level plain over there—so level that you'd think there shouldn't be any mountains—there's this holy mountain: Suleiman Mountain. And if you slaughter sheep at the foot of the mountain and pray to God, then climb up the mountain, bowing and praying to God at every step—and also ask Him very nicely—he can take pity on you and give you a child. Aunt Bekai wants very much to go there, to climb up Suleiman Mountain, but Uncle Orozkul isn't very eager. It's far away. It'll cost lots of money, he says. You can only get there on an airplane over the mountains, after all. And it's very far to the airplane, which also costs money...

When they go off to the city, we're left all alone in the cordon. We and our neighbours—Uncle Seidakhmat and his wife Guljamal and their little daughter. That's all of us there are.

In the evening when all the work's done, grandfather tells me stories. I know that outside it's a pitch-black and freezing cold night. The wind is furious. On those nights even the biggest mountains of all lose heart and push in all together, closer to our house—to the light in our little windows. It makes me frightened and happy. If I were a giant, I'd put on a giant's sheepskin and go out of the house. I'd tell them, the mountains, very loudly: "Don't lose heart, mountains, I'm here. Even if there's a wind, even if it's dark, or there's a snowstorm, I'm not afraid of anything. And don't you be afraid either. Stay in your own places, don't bunch up all together."

Then I'd push through the snowdrifts and step over the river into the forest. Because the trees get terribly frightened at night, alone in the forest. They're all alone and nobody talks to them. The naked trees get a chill in the hard frosts—they've no place for shelter. And I'd walk through the forest and pat each tree on its trunk, so it wouldn't be afraid. Probably the trees that don't go green in spring are ones that were chilled with fear. We cut down these dead ones for firewood.

I think about all this when grandfather tells me tales. He tells long, long ones. He has all kinds—funny ones, especially about the boy the size of a thumb called Chipalak, who the greedy wolf swallowed, to its own grief. No, first he was eaten by a camel. Chipalak fell asleep under a leaf, and the camel wandered near by—and oop! ate him together with the leaf. That's why people say: no camel ever knew, what he did chew. Chipalak began to shout and call for help, and his old parents had to cut open the camel to rescue him.

But what happened to the wolf was even worse. He too swallowed Chipalak because of his own stupidity—and then cried bitter tears. The wolf had stumbled upon Chipalak. "What's this gnat getting in my way? I'll lick you up in a twinkling." But Chipalak said: "Don't you touch me, wolf, or I'll make you into a dog." "Ho ho," the wolf laughed. "Who ever heard of that—a wolf turning into a dog? I'm going to eat you up for your cheek." And he swallowed him. Swallowed and forgot.

But from that moment, his life as a wolf was finished. As soon as he'd start sneaking up on some sheep, Chipalak would cry from inside him "Hey—shepherds... wake up! It's me, the grey wolf sneaking up—to drag off a sheep." The wolf wouldn't know what to do. He'd bite himself in his flanks or roll over on the ground. But this wouldn't stop Chipalak shouting, "Hey, shepherds—run over here. Beat me, flog me!" The shepherds would fall on the wolf with clubs; the wolf would try to flee. The shepherds ran after him, full of wonder and awe. The big bad wolf had gone barmy: although running away, he himself was also shouting. "Catch up to me, dear chaps, beat me, have no pity." The shepherds would collapse with laughter, and at that moment the big bad wolf would take to his heels. But it did him no good. Wherever he poked his nose, Chipalak did him down. He was chased away everywhere and laughed at everywhere. The wolf grew scraggy from hunger; only skin and bones were left. He gnashed his teeth and whined, "What am I being punished for like this? Why am I bringing all hell down on myself? Am I going senile in my old age, going off my whacky mind?" Chipalak would whisper into his ear. "Run over to Tashmat, he's got some plump sheep! Trot down to Bdimat, his dogs are deaf. Go up to Ermat, his shepherds are sleeping." But the wolf would just sit there and snivel: "I'm not going anywhere. The only place I can go is to hire myself out to somebody as a dog."

It's really a funny tale, isn't it, papa? Grandfather has other tales too—unhappy, scary and sad. But my favourite story of all is about Horned Deer-Mother. Grandfather says that everybody who lives on the Issik-Kul should know this story. Not to know it is a sin. Maybe you know it, papa? Grandfather says that every word is true. That it all happened once upon a time. That we're all children of Horned Deer-Mother. You and I and everybody else . . .

That's how we live in winter. Winter drags on for a very long time. If it weren't for grandfather's tales, it would be awfully dull for me in winter.

But it's fine here in spring. When it warms up fully the shepherds come to the mountains again. And then we're not alone in the mountains. Still, nobody lives on the other side of the river, in back of us. Only the forest is there, and everything that lives in the forest. That's why we live on the cordon—so that no one sets foot there, no one touches even a single branch. Even learned people come to visit us. Two women, both in pants, a little old man and also a young man. The young man was their student. They lived here a whole month—gathering all kinds of grasses, leaves and branches. They said that there are very few forests left on earth like ours in San-Tash. You can say there are almost none. Therefore every tree in the forest must be protected.

And I used to think that our grandfather watched over every tree just like that, for no particular reason. He doesn't like it at all when Uncle Orozkul gives away fir trees for building logs.

III

THE WHITE STEAMSHIP steamed away. By this time, you couldn't make out its funnels in the binoculars. Soon it would pass out of sight. It was now time for the lad to make up an ending to his voyage on his father's ship.

Although everything up to this point always came out well, the ending never worked. He could picture quite easily how he turned into a fish and swam downriver, into the lake. How he intercepted the white steamship and met up with his father. And everything he told his father. But after that, things wouldn't hang together. Because, for example, the shore would already be in sight. The ship would be steering for the pier, the sailors getting ready to go ashore. Then they'd all separate to make their way home. Father would have to go home too. His wife and two children would be waiting for him on the pier.

What now? Would he go with his father? Would his papa take him along? If he did, his wife would ask: "Who's that, where did he come from, why is he here?" No, it was better not to go . . .

The white steamship moved farther and farther away, turning into a speck you could hardly see. The sun already lay on the water. In the binoculars, you could see the lake's violet surface blazing blindingly.

The ship moved on and disappeared. That was the end of the tale about the white steamship. He had to go home.

The lad picked up his briefcase from the ground and clutched the binoculars under his arm. He descended from the mountain quickly, running in zigzags down the slope. And the closer he came to home, the more uneasy he felt inside. He had to face answering for the dress that the calf had chewed apart. He was already unable to think of anything except the punishment. So as not to lose heart completely, the lad said to the briefcase: "Don't be afraid. All right, we'll be yelled at. But I didn't do it on purpose, after all. I simply didn't know that the calf had run away. All right, I'll get a slap, I can take it. And if they slam you to the ground, don't be scared. You won't fall apart, you're a briefcase after all. Now if the binoculars fall into old grandma's hands, it won't be so healthy for them—so first we'll hide the binoculars in the shed, then we'll go home."

Which is what he did. And felt frightened to step inside his own house.

But an alarming hush reigned there. In the yard, it was as quiet and empty as if everyone had deserted the entire place. Apparently Aunt Bekai's husband had beaten her again. Once more, it fell to grandfather Momun to soothe his crazed son-in-law—again he had to plead, implore and hang on Orozkul's heavy fists. And to witness the full disgrace of his beaten, dishevelled, wailing daughter. And to hear his daughter cursed in the vilest of vile language and in the presence of her own father. Hear her called a barren bitch, a thrice-cursed desert she-ass and various other terms. And hear his daughter curse her fate in a wild, demented voice. "Am I the one who's guilty if God's kept me from conceiving? Millions of women in the world breed like sheep, yet I'm cursed in heaven. Why? Why was I given this life? I'd rather you killed me, you fiend. Here—beat me, beat away ..."

Old Momun dolefully sat in a corner, still breathing hard. His eyelids were sealed and hands lay slanting on his knee. He was very pale.

Momun glanced at his grandson, said nothing, and again wearily shut his eyes. Old grandma wasn't home. She'd gone to reconcile Aunt Bekai with her husband and to put their house in order and pick up the broken dishes. That's the kind old grandma was: when Orozkul beat his wife, she stayed out of it and kept grandfather out. But after the brawl, she went over to calm them down with good sense. That, at least, was something to be thankful for.

Most of all, the lad felt sorry for the old man. Each time this happened, he sat in the corner as if stunned, hiding himself from everyone. He told no one, not a soul on earth, what he was thinking. During those moments, Momun was thinking that he was already an old man, and that he'd had a single son— who died during the war. Everyone had forgotten him now; no one remembered what he was like. If his son were alive, perhaps his fate would have taken a different turn. Momun pined for his dead wife, with whom he'd lived a whole lifetime. But his deepest grief was brought on by his daughters having drawn unhappy lots. Having plunked her grandson in his lap, the younger one had moved to the city where she lived in misery with a large family in one room. The other one lived a wretched life here with Orozkul. And although he, the old man, was with her and would endure everything for his own daughter's sake, the happiness of motherhood simply eluded her. She'd already spent many years with Orozkul. And was sick to death of her life with him—but where could she go? What would happen in the future? He himself would die any day now; he was an old man, after all. What then would befall his ill-fated daughter?

The lad hurriedly gulped some soured milk from a cup, ate a piece of home-baked bread and settled down very quietly next to the window. He decided not to turn on the light because he didn't want to disturb grandfather. Let him sit in peace there with his thoughts.

The lad was soon deep in his own thoughts. He couldn't understand why Aunt Bekai indulged her husband in vodka. Orozkul responded with his fists — after which she would bring him yet another half-litre.

Oh Aunt Bekai, Aunt Bekai. How many times had her husband beaten her half-dead, yet she always forgave him. And grandfather Momun always forgave him too. But why forgive? People like that shouldn't be forgiven. He's a worthless, nasty man. Nobody needs him here. We'd get along fine without him.

An embittered child's imagination graphically pictured a just punishment in the mind's eye of the lad. They would all pounce upon Orozkul, and drag him, the big, fat, dirty man, to the river. Then, having swung him once or twice, they'd toss him straight into the surf. And he'd beg forgiveness of Aunt Bekai and grandfather Momun. Because *he* couldn't turn into a fish...

The lad felt better. He even found his picture of Orozkul in his dreams funny — floundering in the river, with his corduroy hat floating alongside.

But to his great disappointment, grown-ups didn't behave as the lad thought fair. They always did the opposite. When Orozkul came home tipsy he was greeted as if nothing were wrong. Grandfather would see to his horse and his wife run to set the samovar. All as if everyone had only been waiting for him. Then he'd start throwing his weight around. First he'd be all sad and cry. As if to say, how could it have happened:

every little nobody of a man, the kind people don't even bother to shake hands with, has children to his heart's content. Five, even ten. In what respect was he, Orozkul, worse than any of them? Why didn't things go right for him?

Maybe his job wasn't big enough? But for the love of God, he was the senior warden of a forest preserve. Or perhaps he was some kind of tramp? But gypsies were up to their ears in little gypsies. Or maybe he was some unknown little man whom nobody respected? But he had everything—had made himself all he wanted to be. He had a horse under his saddle and a whip in hand; people greeted him with deference. Then why were other men his age already celebrating their children's wedding—while he did what? Who was he without a son, without seed?

Aunt Bekai would also cry and fuss about for something with which to play up to her husband. She'd get out a hidden half-litre—and she herself would drink, out of sorrow. Time would pass and the bottle would empty steadily—until suddenly Orozkul would turn brutal and vent all his malice on her, his own wife. And she'd forgive everything. Grandfather forgave everything too. No one put ropes on Orozkul. By morning, he would be sobered up and his wife, although black and blue, would have set the samovar. Grandfather would already have fed and saddled his horse. Orozkul drank his fill of tea, sat on his horse—and again he was a big boss, master of all the San-Tash forests. And no one figured out that somebody like Orozkul should have been thrown into the river long ago.

It was dark now. Night had come to the cordon.

So ended the day when the lad was bought his first school briefcase.

Preparing for bed, he couldn't think of a place for the briefcase. Finally he put it next to himself at the head of the bed. The lad didn't yet know, he'd learn only later, that half his classmates would have exactly the same briefcase. But this wouldn't upset him in the slightest; his briefcase would remain extraordinary, an absolutely singular briefcase. He also didn't know that new events in his young life awaited him, that a day would come when he'd remain alone in the whole wide world, and only the briefcase would remain with him. The cause of all this would be his favourite tale about Horned Deer-Mother...

That evening he yearned to hear this tale again. Old Momun himself loved the story and always told it—sighing, crying, going silent and thinking his own thoughts—as if he himself had witnessed all of it.

However the lad decided not to disturb his grandfather. He understood that he wasn't up to telling tales. "We'll ask him some other time," the boy said to the briefcase. "But now I'll tell about Horned Deer-Mother myself, word for word, just as grandfather does. I'll tell everything so softly that nobody will hear us, but you listen. I like to tell and see everything like in a film. So listen carefully. Grandfather says that it's all true. It all happened..."

IV

It took place long ago. Once upon a time, when the earth had more forest than grass and, where we live, more water than dry land, a Kirghiz tribe lived on the banks of a great, cold river. The river was named the Enesai. It flowed from where we are to very far away, in Siberia. It took three years and three months to gallop there on a horse. Now people call this river the Yenisei, but in those days it was called the Enesai. Which is the reason for this song:

> Is there a river wider than you, Enesai,
> Is there a land dearer than yours, Enesai?
> Is there a sorrow deeper than yours, Enesai,
> Is there a freedom freer than yours, Enesai?
>
> No river is wider than you, Enesai,
> No land is dearer than yours, Enesai.
> No sorrow is deeper than yours, Enesai,
> No freedom is freer than yours, Enesai.

That's the kind of river it was, the Enesai.

Many people lived on the Enesai in those days. Life was hard for them because they were constantly fighting. The Kirghiz tribe was surrounded by many enemies. First one of them attacked, then another, then the Kirghizians themselves went out to raid other tribes, steal their cattle, set fire to their tents, and kill people. They killed everybody they could — that's how it was in those times. Nobody cared about anybody else. Everybody annihilated everybody else. It got so bad that there was nobody to sow wheat, raise cattle or go hunting. It was easier to live by plundering: men would come, kill, and steal. And you had to pay for blood with even more blood; for vengeance, with even more vengeance. As time passed, more and more blood flowed. People were at their wits' end. There was nobody to make peace among the enemies. The man who was able to take his enemy by surprise was considered the wisest and best — who could slaughter another tribe to the last soul, and seize its cattle and riches.

Then a strange bird appeared in the taiga. She sang and wept all night until dawn in a mournful human voice, flying from one branch to another and repeating over and over: "Great grief will come. Great grief will come." Which is exactly what happened; that fearful day dawned.

On that day, the Kirghiz tribe on the Enesai was burying their old chief. *Batir** Kulche had been the tribe's leader for many years; he fought in many campaigns and wielded his sword and sabre in many battles. Although he had survived all the fierce fighting, the hour of his death struck. His tribesmen were in the deepest mourning for two days, and assembled on the third to commit the *batir*'s remains to the earth. According to the old custom, the leader's body was to be taken on its last journey down the banks of the Enesai and along the precipice and steeps, so that the soul of the deceased might take leave of the mother-river.

* *Batir*: a Central Asian term for a great leader with knight-like qualities.

Because 'Ene' is 'mother', and 'sai' means river-bed. So that his soul could sing the song about the Enesai for the last time.

> Is there a river wider than you, Enesai,
> Is there a land dearer than yours, Enesai?
> Is there a sorrow deeper than yours, Enesai,
> Is there a freedom freer than yours, Enesai?
>
> No river is wider than you, Enesai,
> No land is dearer than yours, Enesai.
> No sorrow is deeper than yours, Enesai,
> No freedom is freer than yours, Enesai.

Having reached the funeral mound, it was the custom to raise the *batir* overhead at the open grave, to show him the four corners of the earth. "Here is your river, here is your sky. Here is your land, and here are we, who are descended from one root with you. We have all come to see you off. Sleep in peace." As a memorial for countless generations of the *batir*'s descendants, a boulder was placed on his grave.

On the day of the funeral, the *yurts* of the entire tribe were arranged in a row on the bank so that each family might take leave of the *batir* at their own threshold. The leave-taking was performed as the body was carried towards the grave. At each *yurt*, a white flag of mourning would be lowered to the ground amidst wailing and lamenting; then the entire procession would proceed to the next *yurt*, where weeping and bewailing would again resound as the white flag of mourning was lowered. This would continue to the very end of the journey, at the burial mound itself.

On the morning of that day, the sun had already commenced its daily journey when all the preparations were completed. Lances with horse-tails were set out on wooden pikestaffs and the *batir*'s armour, his shield and spear, was set out on display.

His horse was covered with a funeral blanket. The trumpeters prepared to sound their battle trumpets, the drummers to play their double-bass drums so that the taiga would shake. So that the birds would take wing in one flock to the heavens and circle about with a chorus of moans; so that the beasts would charge through the thickets, snorting savagely. So that the grasses would flatten themselves to the earth. So that the echo would rumble in the mountains and the mountains themselves shudder. The mourners let down their hair to sanctify *batir* Kulche with their tears. The *dzhigits* lowered themselves to one knee to raise the mortal remains on their powerful shoulders. Everyone was alert and ready, waiting for the *batir* to be borne out on his last journey. And at the forest's edge stood nine sacrificial mares on tethers, nine sacrificial bulls, and nine times nine sacrificial sheep for the funeral repast.

But then something totally unexpected happened. However hostile the peoples of the Enesai were towards each other, it was not customary to go to war with neighbours on the day of a leader's funeral. But at dawn, a horde of enemies had stealthily surrounded the Kirghiz encampment which was immersed in its sorrow. Now they charged from their cover on all sides so that no one had time to mount his horse, even pick up his weapon. A slaughter without parallel began. One after another, every last person was killed. This was precisely the enemy's scheme: to have done with the impudent Kirghiz tribe at a single blow. They killed one and all, so that no one would survive to remember the atrocity; no one to take vengeance. So that time would erase all traces of the past, like dry sand. All this happened—yet didn't . . .

A man takes a long time to be born and to grow up, but killing him is the quickest thing in the world. Many were already slashed to pieces and drowning in pools of blood; many plunged into the river to save themselves from the swords and spears, but drowned in the Enesai's waves. And for miles up and down the bank and along the steeps and precipices, Kirghiz tents burned, embraced by roaring flames. No one managed to escape; no one survived. Everything was ravaged and burned to the ground. The bodies of the fallen were thrown from the crest atop the bank into the river. The enemy rejoiced in triumph. "Now these are our lands! Now these are our forests! Now these are our herds!"

The enemy withdrew with its rich booty and did not notice two children returning from the forest: a little boy and little girl. Disobedient and naughty, they had secretly sneaked away from their parents in the morning, entering the nearest forest to gather bark to make baskets. Absorbed in play, they did not notice how deep they had wandered into the core of the forest. But when they heard the din and shouts of the slaughter, they rushed back—to find neither their fathers nor mothers alive, neither their sisters nor their brothers. The children were left without kith or kin. They ran weeping from ruin to smouldering ruin—but not a soul survived anywhere. In a single hour they had become orphans. In the whole world, they alone survived. But a cloud of dust swirled in the distance, where the enemy was driving the flocks and herds seized in their gory raid towards their own lands.

The children saw the dust raised by hoofs and hurried in pursuit. Bathed in tears and calling loudly, they ran after the rabid enemy. Only children could have behaved that way: instead of hiding from the killers, they set out to overtake them. Anything not to remain alone, anything to get away from the cursed site of the massacre. Hand in hand, the little boy and little girl ran after the bandits' train begging for them to wait, to be taken with them. But who could hear their feeble voices amidst the din, neighing and thudding hoofs of the train's tempestuous homeward march?

For a long time, the boy and girl ran in desperation. But they never caught up. Finally they fell to the ground. They were terrified to look around them, terrified even to move. Horror gripped them. They pressed closer to one another and didn't notice that they had fallen asleep.

Not for nothing it's said that orphans have seven lives. The night passed safely. No animals fell on them, no forest creatures dragged them away. When they awoke, it was morning; the sun was shining and birds singing. The children got up and again dragged themselves along the trail of the enemy's column. They gathered berries and roots along the way. They walked and walked, and on the third day stopped on a mountain. They looked about, and down below, on a wide green meadow, a great feast and revel was taking place. *Yurt* beyond count had been set up there; camp fires beyond count were smoking; people beyond count were gathered around the camp fires. Young girls swung on swings and sang songs. Athletic warriors were performing for the crowd, circling for position and flinging one another to the ground. This is the way that the enemy was celebrating its victory.

Lacking the nerve to descend, the boy and girl stood on the mountain. But they yearned to find themselves around the camp fires where it smelled so deliciously of skewered meat, bread and wild onions.

Unable to hold out, the children began climbing down from the mountain. Amazed, the local tribesmen surrounded them in a mob.

"Who are you? Where did you come from?"

"We're hungry," answered the boy and girl. "Give us something to eat."

The tribesmen guessed who they were by their speech, and this caused a great stir. They began to argue: should the surviving enemy seed be killed on the spot, or taken to the khan. While they argued, a certain tender-hearted woman managed to slip each of the children a piece of boiled horse-meat. Although dragged to the khan himself, they could not tear themselves away from their food. They were led to a tall red *yurt* which had guards with silver axes standing outside.

Meanwhile, the disturbing news that children of the Kirghiz tribe had somehow appeared from unknown places spread through the encampment. What could this mean? Everyone dropped his games, abandoned the feast, and ran in a huge crowd to the khan's tent. At that moment, the khan was sitting with his leading warriors in a state of solemnity on a great cushion of snow-white felt. He was drinking mare's milk sweetened with honey and listening to songs of praise. When the khan learned what had brought the crowds to him, he fell into a terrible fury. "How dare you disturb me? Can it be true that we did not exterminate the Kirghiz tribe? Haven't I made you masters of the Enesai forever? Why have you come running here, you cowardly mortals? Take a look at who stands before you! You there—Lame Pock-marked Old Woman," shouted the khan. And when a lame woman had stepped forward from the crowd, he gave her his orders. "Take them into the taiga, and make sure there that the Kirghiz tribe expires with them, that no trace of them remains, that its name is obliterated forever and ever. Be on your way, Lame Pock-marked Old Woman, do as I command . . ."

Lame Pock-marked Old Woman obeyed silently, taking the boy and girl by the hand and leading them away. They walked a great distance through the forest, emerging at last on a high crest over a bank of the Enesai. Here Lame Pock-marked Old Woman patted the little children and stood them side by side on the edge of the precipice. But before she pushed them down, she uttered:

"Oh great river Enesai. If a mountain were thrown into your depths, it would vanish like a stone. If a hundred-year pine tree were thrown, you would carry it away like a chip. Take into your waters two little grains of sand — two children of the human race. There is no place for them on earth. Is it for me to tell you why, Enesai? If the stars became people, there would not be enough sky for them. If fish became people, there would be too few rivers and seas. Is it for me to tell you why, Enesai? Take them and sweep them away. Let them leave our hateful world in their childhood, with pure souls and the conscience of younglings, unsullied by evil intentions and evil deeds. So that they will never know mankind's suffering and themselves will never bring torture to others. Take them, take them, great Enesai . . ."

The boy and girl sobbed and wept. What could an old woman's speeches mean to them when it was terrifying to glance down from the precipice? Far below, the waves surged violently.

"Embrace each other, my children, say farewell for the last time," said Lame Pock-marked Old Woman. She rolled up her sleeves, the easier to throw them from the precipice. "And now, forgive me, my children," she said. "This is what fate has decided, you understand. Although I am not doing this of my own will, still it is for your own good . . ."

Hardly had she said these words when a voice rang out from near by.

"Hold on, great wise woman, do not murder innocent children."

Lame Pock-marked Old Woman turned around, looked, and gave in to awe. Before her stood a doe: a great maral* dam. And what enormous eyes it had, now filled with reproach and sorrow. The doe herself was white like a young mother's first milk, and her belly was lined with a tannish fur as on a young camel. The horns were a work of beauty, spreading outward like boughs of autumn trees. And her udders were smooth and clean, like the breasts of a nursing mother.

* Maral: a species of deer found principally in Siberia.

"Who are you? Why do you speak in the language of men?" asked Lame Pock-marked Old Woman.

"I'm Deer-Mother," she answered. "And I spoke that way because otherwise you would not have understood me, and not heeded."

"What do you want, Deer-Mother?"

"Let the children go, great wise woman. I ask it of you: give them to me."

"What need have you of them?"

"People have killed my brood, two younglings. I'm trying to find children for myself."

"You want to rear them?"

"Yes, great wise woman."

"Have you thought carefully, Deer-Mother?" said Lame Pock-marked Old Woman with a laugh. "Remember, they are human children. They'll grow up and kill your own fawns."

"When they grow up, they will do no such thing as kill my fawns," the mother-maral answered. "I will be a mother to them, and they will be my children. Would they really do such a thing as kill their own brothers and sisters?"

"Oh don't you believe it, Deer-Mother—you don't know how people are." Lame Pock-marked Old Woman shook her head. "They're not like the creatures of the forest: they have no pity for one another. I'd give you the little orphans so that you yourself might learn that my words are true. But people would kill even these of your children. Why would you want so much grief?"

"I will take the children away to distant parts, where no one will find them. Have pity on the little ones, great wise woman; let them go. I will be a faithful mother to them. My udders are overflowing. My milk cries out for children. My milk begs for children."

"Well, well, if that's how it is," said Lame Pock-marked Old Woman, having made her decision. "Take them quickly and lead them away. Lead the orphans away to your distant parts. But if they die on the long journey, if they are killed by brigands who cross your path, if your human children repay you with black ingratitude — you have only yourself to blame."

Deer-Mother thanked Lame Pock-marked Old Woman. Then she spoke to the little boy and girl.

"Now I am your mother and you are my children. I will lead you to a distant land where, amidst snowy forested mountains, lies a hot sea — the Issik-Kul."

The boy and girl rejoiced and ran friskily after Horned Deer-Mother. But soon they grew tired and weak; and the journey was long — from one corner of the earth to the other. They would not have gone far had not Horned Deer-Mother nursed them with her milk and warmed them at night with her body. They travelled a great distance. Their old Enesai homeland was left farther and farther behind, but it was still very far to the new homeland on the Issik-Kul. Summer and winter, spring and summer, autumn and again summer and winter, again spring, again summer and autumn — during all these seasons they made their way across dense forests and burning steppes, through quicksand, over high mountains and across raging rivers. Packs of wolves pursued them, but placing the children on her back, Horned Deer-Mother saved them from the fierce animals. Hunters on horseback and with arrows chased them, crying, "The doe has stolen human children. Stop her! Catch her!" — and shot their arrows in pursuit. But from them too, from all unbidden rescuers, Horned Deer-Mother saved the children. She ran faster than the arrows, whispering simply: "Hold on tighter, my children. They're after us!"

At last Horned Deer-Mother delivered her children to the Issik-Kul. They stood on the mountain and marvelled. Snowy crests towered everywhere around them and amidst the mountains covered with green forests as far as the eye could see, splashed and sparkled the great sea. White waves moved across the blue water; the wind whipped them from far behind and drove them far away. No one could tell where the Issik-Kul began and where it ended. The sun rose at one end while at the other it was still night. Mountains beyond count soared around the Issik-Kul, nor could one guess how many of the same snowy peaks stood beyond these mountains.

"This is your new homeland," said Horned Deer-Mother. "You will live here—will farm the earth, catch fish and raise cattle. You will live here in peace for a thousand years. Your kin will endure and multiply. And your descendants will not forget the tongue which you have brought here; let them take delight in talking and singing in their own language. Live as human beings should live. And I shall be with you and your children from now and forever . . ."

This is how the boy and girl, the last of the Kirghiz tribe, found a new homeland on the blessed and eternal Issik-Kul.

Time passed quickly. The boy became a strong man and the girl a mature woman. Then they were married and became man and wife. Horned Deer-Mother did not leave the Issik-Kul but lived in the neighbouring forests.

One day at dawn, the Issik-Kul suddenly ran high and made a great clamour. Labour had come to the woman; she was in pain. The man was frightened. He ran atop a cliff and began calling loudly.

"Where are you, Horned Deer-Mother? Do you hear the clamour the Issik-Kul is making? Your daughter is giving birth. Come quickly, Horned Deer-Mother—help us . . ."

Then a lilting peal was heard from afar, like the tinkling of a caravan bell. The pealing came closer and closer; finally Horned Deer-Mother ran into sight. She carried a child's cradle on her horns, hooked under its arch—a *beshik*. The *beshik* was made of white birchwood, and a silver bell jingled on its arch. To this day, that bell jingles on Issik-Kul *beshiks*.

Mothers rock their cradles and the silver bell tinkles, as if Horned Deer-Mother is running up from afar, hastening to bring a birch cradle on her horns . . .

The moment Horned Deer-Mother appeared to answer the call for her the woman gave birth.

"This *beshik* is for your first-born," said Horned Deer-Mother. "You will have many children—seven sons and seven daughters."

The mother and father rejoiced. They named their first-born in honour of Horned Deer-Mother—Bugubai. Bugubai grew up, took a beauty from the Kipchak tribe as his bride, and the Bugu clan—the clan of Horned Deer-Mother—began to multiply. The Bugu clan became great and strong on the Issik-Kul. The Buguans revered Horned Deer-Mother as their goddess. An emblem was embroidered at the entrance to Buguan *yurts*: maral horns, so that it would be seen from afar that the *yurt* belonged to the Bugu clan. When the Buguans repulsed enemy raids and competed in games on horseback, the war cry "To Bugu" resounded—and they emerged victorious. In those days, white, horned marals roamed the Issik-Kul forests, and the stars in the sky envied their beauty. They were Horned Deer-Mother's offspring. No one disturbed them; no one allowed them to be hurt. At the sight of a maral, the Buguans dismounted and made way for her. They compared the beauty of their favourite young girls with the white marals' beauty . . .

This was how life went on until the death of a very rich, very famous Buguan—he had had a thousand thousand sheep and a thousand thousand horses, and everyone near by had served as his shepherd. His sons organised a great funeral feast for him, inviting the most celebrated people from all corners of the earth to his feast. They set up a thousand and one hundred *yurts* for the guests on the shore of the Issik-Kul. No one could count how many cattle were slaughtered, how much mare's milk was drunk, how many kashgar sweets* were served. The sons of the rich man carried themselves with an air of great importance: people should know what rich and generous heirs survived the dead man, how they respected him and cherished his memory... ("Beware, my son, it's a bad sign when people make a display not of wisdom but of wealth!")

The bards, riding about on thoroughbred horses that the sons of the deceased had given them and showing off in sable hats and silk gowns, also provided for them, vied with each other to praise the deceased and his heirs.

"Where else under the sun can you see such a happy life, such a luxurious feast?" sang one.

"From the day of the earth's creation, nothing like this has taken place!" sang a second.

"No one else but we revere our parents, render homage to our parents' honour and glory, cherish their sacred names," sang a third.

"Hey you gas-bags, what are you chirping about here? Do you really think that words worthy of these bounties exist? Are there any words equal to the deceased's glory?" sang a fourth...

Thus they competed day and night. ("Beware, my son, it's a bad sign when bards compete in this kind of eulogising. Singers turn into enemies of song.")

The memorable funeral feast was celebrated for many days, each like a holiday. The rich man's conceited sons wanted dearly to outshine all others and surpass everyone else on earth, so that word of them would spread through the entire world. And they thought to mount a maral's horns on the tomb of their father, so that everyone would know that this was the final resting place of their renowned ancestor of the clan of Horned Deer-Mother. ("Beware, my son: as long ago as

---

* Kashgar sweet: named after the Chinese city of Kashgar, this is one of the 'eastern sweets' popular in Central Asia.

ancient times, people said that wealth breeds arrogance—and arrogance, recklessness.")

Once the sons of the plutocrat felt the wish to bestow this unheard-of honour upon their father's memory, nothing held them back. It was no sooner said than done. They dispatched hunters, and the hunters slew a maral and felled her horns. The horns were magnificent, like the wings of an eagle taking flight. The sons were duly pleased with the maral's horns, each of which had eighteen shoots—meaning the deer had lived eighteen years. Fine work! They ordered craftsmen to mount the horns on the tomb.

Old men at the feast were indignant.

"By what right did they kill a maral? Who dared raise his hand to the offspring of Horned Deer-Mother?"

The heirs of the rich man answered.

"The maral was killed on our territory. And everything that walks, crawls and flies in our domain, from flies to camels, is ours. We know how to deal with our own possessions. Be off with you."

Servants beat the old men with lashes, mounted them backwards on horses and banished them in disgrace.

It all began with this. Great misfortune befell the progeny of Horned Deer-Mother. Almost everyone began hunting white marals in the forests. Every Buguan considered it his duty to mount maral horns on the graves of his ancestors. Now this practice was regarded as something virtuous, as a token of special respect to the memory of the dead. Those who couldn't lay hands on horns were now considered unworthy. A trade in maral horns sprang up, and they were laid in store. People emerged from the clan of Horned Deer-Mother who made their craft acquiring maral horns and selling them for money. ("Beware, my son, where money rules, there is no place for a kind word, no place for beauty.")

Dark days befell the marals of the Issik-Kul forests. They

were shown no mercy. The marals took refuge in inaccessible cliffs, but were hunted down even there. Packs of hound dogs were let loose upon them, driving the marals into the ambush of hunters, who felled them with rarely a miss. Marals were killed in entire herds; they were flushed out in whole stands. Bets were laid as to who would get the horns with the most shoots.

Finally, no marals remained. The mountains had been emptied. Not at midnight nor at dawn could a maral be heard. Not in forest nor glade could one be seen grazing, galloping, tossing his horns on his back or leaping over a crevasse, like a bird in flight. People were born who would never see a maral during their entire lives. They only heard fairy-tales about them — yes, and saw horns on tombs.

And what happened to Horned Deer-Mother?

She was deeply hurt and took grave offence against people. It was said that when bullets and hound dogs had made life impossible for the marals, when maral had become so few that you could easily count them on your fingers, Horned Deer-Mother mounted the very highest mountain peak, bade farewell to the Issik-Kul and led her last children across a great pass, to another land and other mountains.

These are the kind of things that can happen on earth. This is the full tale — believe it if you want to; if not, don't.

When Horned Deer-Mother left, she said that it was never to return . . .

V

Autumn had come again to the mountains. After the bustling summer, everything prepared itself once more for autumn's silence. The dust of cattle drives had settled all around and the camp fires been extinguished. The herds had left for winter. People too had left. The mountains were emptied.

Now eagles were flying on high, keeping to their solitude and sparing of their cries. The rumble of the river's waters had become more hollow: in summer, the river had grown accustomed to its bed, wearing its way in and becoming more and more shallow. The grass had stopped growing and faded through to its roots. The leaves tired of clinging to their branches and steadily fell. And silvery young snow already covered the highest peak at night. Towards morning, the dark ridges of its crests turned grey, like the manes of silver fox.

The wind in the canyons grew sharper and colder. But so far, the days were still dry and bright.

The forests across the river, opposite the cordon, quickly succumbed to autumn. From the river upwards—up to the border of Black Pine Forest—autumn's foliage raged like a smokeless fire through the steep thickets of smaller trees. The loudest colours of all were gingers and crimsons; the most tenacious in growing on the steep ascent were the aspen and birch groves, which reached up to the heights of the great forest itself—to the kingdom of gloomy firs and pines, lying just beneath the snows.

As always, it was chaste and severe in the forest, as in a temple. Nothing but hard, brown trunks, nothing but a dry resinous smell, nothing but umber needles packed densely about the forest's feet. Nothing but wind coursing inaudibly among the crowns of old pine trees.

But today, agitated jackdaws had been generating a steady din over the mountains since morning. Screaming furiously, a large flock circled incessantly over the pine forest. The jackdaws had taken alarm immediately upon hearing the thud of axes. Now, vying with each other in screeching as if being robbed in broad daylight, they pursued two men who were hauling a recently cut pine log down the mountain.

The log was being dragged on a chain hitched to a horse's harness. Orozkul trod in front, leading the horse by the bridle. Tensed like a bull, his raincoat catching on the bushes, he clumped down like an ox ploughing a furrow. In back of him, behind the log, grandfather Momun kept up with the pace. He too found the going hard at this height; the old man gasped for breath. He grasped a birch lever in his hand, using it to hook under the log as he climbed down. The log kept lodging on stumps and rocks, and in the steep places would try to swing around sideways to the slope and roll straight down. If this happened, disaster was inevitable: the men would be crushed to death.

The man who controlled the log with the lever was in the most dangerous position—but you could never tell: Orozkul had already leapt away from the harness several times. And each time was seared with shame when he saw the old man risking his life to restrain the log on the slope and waiting until Orozkul would return to the horse and take its bridle. And it's not for nothing that people say: to hide your own disgrace, you must disgrace someone else.

"What are you trying to do—finish me off?" Orozkul screamed at his father-in-law.

No one was near them to overhear this and condemn Orozkul, for it was unheard of to treat an elderly man this way. Timidly, the father-in-law remarked that he too, after all, might have fallen under the log. Why shout at him that way, as if he'd arranged it all purposely?

But this nettled Orozkul still more.

"Phoo, what a character you are," he said with great indignation. "If you're mashed to pieces—okay, you've lived out your time. What does it matter to you? But if I'm smashed up, who'll take your daughter? Who needs her, that barren thing? Barren as a wizard's whip . . ."

"You're a hard man, my son," was Momun's answer. "You don't have any respect for people."

Orozkul stopped short and measured the old man with his gaze. "Old duffers like you should have been sitting around the fire long ago, warming their arses on the ashes. You get your wages, don't you?—such as they are. Where do they come from, those wages? Through me. What other kind of respect do you need?"

"All right, all right—I just said it by the by," said Momun with resignation.

They pushed on in this manner. After mastering another rise, they stopped for a rest on the slope. The horse was soaked in foam. But the jackdaws did not take this occasion to quiet themselves. They kept circling as before: thousands of them, all making a din as if they'd set themselves the goal to scream all day today, and do nothing else but scream.

"They scent an early winter," said Momun to change the subject and dampen Orozkul's anger. "They're bunching up for migration. They don't like it when they're disturbed," he added, as if apologising for the unreasonable birds.

"Who's disturbing them?" said Orozkul, turning around sharply. Suddenly he went crimson. "Watch what you say, old man," he warned in a low but threatening voice.

"Phoo," he thought, "what's the old one driving at? What are we supposed to do—not touch a tree because of his jackdaws, not break a branch? I'm not having any of that. So far at least, I'm in charge here." He clapped an angry eye on the screeching flock.

"If I only had a machine gun, damn it," he said. And turning away, he swore obscenely.

Momun said nothing. He needed no adjustment to his son-in-law's swearing. "He's out of his senses again," the old man said sadly to himself. "He turns into some kind of animal when he drinks. And when he's in one of his hangovers, you can't say anything to him either. What makes people like that?" Momun grieved. "You do him a good turn, and he answers with malice. And he's ashamed of nothing, he never thinks better of things. As if that's the way things should be. He thinks he's right. As long as he gets the best of everything. Everybody else must wait on him. If you don't want to—he'll make you. It's still bearable when his kind is off in the mountains or forests and has only a couple of people at his disposal. But what if he turns up in some higher post somewhere? God forbid! That kind of person is always around. Always grabbing for themselves. And you can never escape from his kind. They're waiting for you everywhere, hunting for you. They'll stop at nothing in the way they treat you so that they can live their soft lives. And make out that they're right, of course. Yes, that kind of person's always around . . ."

"All right, you've stood around long enough," Orozkul

interrupted the old man's reflections. "Let's get going," he ordered. And they moved on.

Orozkul had been in a bad mood since early morning. In the morning, when they'd had to cross over the the opposite bank and into the forest with the equipment, Momun hurried to take his grandson to school. He'd gone completely senile! Every morning he saddled the horse, took the boy to school — then galloped over again to bring him home from school. All that fuss over an abandoned kid, the side-effect of a night's pleasure. You'd think the kid couldn't be late for school. Here we are working on something that only God knows how will turn out — and we're supposed to just drop it and wait around? That's what he supposes? "I'll be back in a flash," he says. "If the boy's late for class it's embarrassing in front of the teacher." He found the right one to be embarrassed in front of, that fool!

Who the hell is she anyway, that teacher? She's been going around in the same overcoat for five years. Always loaded down with notebooks and shopping bags ... And thumbing rides on the road to the district centre because she's always needing something there, something's always lacking. First coal for the school, then glass for the windows, next it's chalk or even dust rags. To think that any self-respecting teacher would work in a school like that! The name they thought up for it: Mini School. You bet it's runty all right. And good for what? All the teachers worth anything at all were in the city. With schools made of glass. Teachers in ties. But that's in the city ... where the bosses sit around on the back seats and are driven through the streets. And what cars! They make you feel like stopping and standing up to attention until they glide past. Black, smooth, sparkling cars. And all the city folk act as if they don't even notice them; they've got no time because they're always dashing somewhere. That's real life for you — over there, in the city. That's where a man should shove on to and get himself fixed with a good job. City people know how to respect a man according to his job. That's what's expected: people can't get away with not showing respect. The higher the job, the more respect. Civilised people. And just because you've sat at somebody's table or accepted some kind of gift, you don't have to drag logs about or anything like that. Not like here—somebody gives you fifty roubles or maybe a century with a real push—and for that he's got to cart away his timber. Who knows, he can even slap a complaint against you. 'Bribe-taker Orozkul,' he'll call you, he's this kind or that . . . Plain ignorance!

Yeah, to be in the city! To goddam hell with all these mountains and forests, these filthy logs. And that empty-wombed wife and this brainless old geezer with his bastard kid who he fusses over like some kind of wonder. Ekh, I'd love to cut loose, like a horse full up on oats. I'd make them respect me . . . "Orozkul Balazhanovich, may I please step into your office?"

And he'd marry a city girl there. Why not? Say some entertainer—a real beauty who sang and maybe danced a bit with a microphone in her hand. They say what that kind cares about is a man who holds down a big job. He'd take one of those beauties by the arm—and he himself would be dressed up fine. Then off to a film. She'd clack away on her high heels and smell of perfume. Passers-by would sniff at her. Before you knew it, there'd be children. He'd see to it that his son became a lawyer, and his little girl would play the piano. You can always spot city children at a glance—because they're smart. They speak only Russian at home, instead of stuffing their heads with village lingo. That's the way he'd bring up his own kids. "Daddy, Mummy, I'd like this, may I have that . . ." Can anyone really begrudge something to his own offspring? Oh, he'd get the better of lots of people, he'd show them who he was. He was as good as anybody else. The people at the top

—who were they, in what way better than him? They were just people, people like him. They happened to be lucky. But not him. Luck evaded him. But it was his own fault too. He should have gone to the city after his forestry course and applied for a technical school or even an institute. He'd been impatient; he yearned for an official position. Even a minor one, so long as it was an official position. So now he had to traipse around some mountains, dragging logs back and forth like a donkey ... And jackdaws to top it all off. What the hell were they shouting for? Why were they circling around? Ekh, if he only had a machine gun ...

Orozkul had cause to be upset. He'd had a fine time all summer. Autumn approached, and together with summer, the days of his eating and drinking as the shepherds' and herders' guest departed. As the song goes, "When the blossoms fade on the mountain meadows, it's time to be leaving for the lowlands ..."

Autumn had arrived. Now Orozkul had to pay for the honour accorded him, for his food and drink, his promises and debts. As well as for his bragging. "What do you need? Only two pine logs for beams? It's not worth even mentioning. Come on over and you can cart them away."

He had talked a lot of hot air, accepted tributes, drank much vodka. And now—panting, drenched in sweat and cursing everything on earth—he was yanking these whopping logs around the mountains. The whole deal turned out to be a miserable mess for him. And his whole life in general was a mess. Suddenly a desperate thought flashed across his mind: "I'll spit on all this and get out. Just leave for wherever my fancy takes me." But he realised immediately that he would go nowhere. He was no use to anyone anywhere, and wouldn't find the life he wanted for himself anywhere either.

Just try to leave this place or renege on your promises! His own cronies would give him away. People weren't worth a damn these days. The year before last, he'd promised a Buguan, his own kinsman, a pine log in return for the gift of a young lamb. But in the autumn, he didn't feel like crawling up the mountain to search for the tree. It's easy enough to say, but just try to climb up there—then saw through the thing and carry it down. And if, on top of this, the tree's lived on this earth more than a decade—try and mess around with it. All the gold in the world couldn't make you want to tackle it. At that very time, old Momun was sick in bed. You couldn't cope alone—nobody's ever coped alone with a full-grown pine log in the mountains. You could fell it all right—and he *would* fell the pine. But not get it down the slopes. If he'd known in advance what was going to happen, he'd have gone after the tree with Seidakhmat.

Too lazy to clamber up the mountain, Orozkul decided to get his kinsman off his back with the first piece of timber that turned up. But the man wouldn't give in: hand over his genuine pine log, and not a damn thing less. "You know how to grab a young lamb, all right—but can't keep your word?" Orozkul went into a rage and tossed him out of his house: you don't like what I offer—then scram. But this fellow knew his way around. He scribbled an official complaint against the inspector of the San-Tash forest preserve, Orozkul Balazhanovich. He painted such a picture, full of fact and fiction, that Orozkul might as well have been shot as a 'wrecker of socialist forests'. Orozkul was dragged through an endless series of investigating committees from the district centre and the Ministry of Forests. He pulled through only by the skin of his teeth ... That's a relative for you! And on top of it, that particular one liked to say that "we're all the children of Horned Deer-Mother. All for one and one for all." All that's pure bullshit—and what the hell does some deer count for when everybody's poised to grab for your jugular for a kopek, or clap you in jail? It was in prehistoric times when people believed in some kind of deer. There was no end to the stupidity and ignorance in those days — it was plain ridiculous. Now, on the other hand, everybody was civilised and literate. Who needs those babyish fairy-tales?

After that episode, Orozkul swore solemnly that he would never again give a branch or a twig to anybody. Not to any acquaintances and not to a single fellow tribesman, even if they were the children of Horned Deer-Mother three times over.

But summer returned. White *yurts* appeared on the green mountain meadows. Herds began to bray and puffs of smoke to trail out from alongside brooks and rivers. The sun shone and it smelled of flowers and of intoxicating mare's milk. It was good to sit around in the open air, on the green grass near the *yurts* and in the company of old acquaintances. And to savour mare's milk and the meat of young lambs. And then to gulp a glass of vodka and feel giddy in the noggin — feel that you could tear a tree out by its roots or wring the head off that mountain over there ... During those days, Orozkul forgot his vow. It was delicious to hear himself called a great lord of a great forest. And once again he made promises and accepted tributes. Once again one of the forest's rare old pines didn't suspect that from the first signs of autumn, its days were numbered.

From the reaped fields, autumn stole unnoticed into the mountains and began to poke about in all directions. The grass turned auburn in the places where she broke through, together with the leaves in the forest.

The berries ripened and lambs matured. They were divided into flocks, young ewes and young rams separately. The women stored away dried cheese in bags for keeping through the winter. The men assembled to decide who would be first to start the return trip to the valleys. But before leaving, those who had come to an agreement with Orozkul during the summer warned him that on a certain day at a certain hour, they would arrive at the cordon in lorries to collect the timber that had been promised them.

This very evening a lorry with a trailer would come to haul away two pine logs. One was already down below, already floated across the river and delivered to the place where the lorry would drive up. As for the second—well, here it was, the one they were now dragging below. If Orozkul could now go back and, speaking plainly, upchuck all he'd eaten and drunk for these logs, he'd go it in a flash; anything to shake off the work and agony he was now forced to endure.

Alas, there was no way to change his damned life in the mountains: the lorry with the trailer would arrive this evening, to haul away the logs at night.

It was still bearable if everything would work out safely; but the road ran through the state farm, right near the checkpoint. There was no other route, and sometimes the police dropped in on the state farm unexpectedly. Or motor vehicle inspectors or other officials from the administrative centre could turn up there at any time. They'd clap eyes on the logs under transport, then start questioning. "Where's that lumber from, where are you hauling it?"

Orozkul's spine tingled at this thought. And he boiled up with spite towards everyone and everything: towards the cawing jackdaws overhead, towards miserable old Momun, towards Seidakhmat, the lazy slob who'd got wise enough three days ago to push off to the city to sell the potatoes. Because he knew that they had to pull some logs down from the mountains. He'd sneaked out of it, as it turned out, and now he'd return only after finishing with every last bit of business in the market. If it weren't for this, Orozkul would have ordered him to drag the logs down together with the old man; he wouldn't have had to go through all this damn trouble himself.

But Seidakhmat was far away, and there was also nothing

to reach the jackdaws with. For lack of anything else, he could always bash his wife around—but it was still a long way home. That left old Momun. Breathing hard, growing more and more furious because of the thinness of the mountain air, cursing at every step, Orozkul tramped straight through the bushes, caring nothing either for the horse or the old man following behind him. Let the horse drop dead, let the old man drop dead —let he himself drop dead of a heart attack. Let the whole world sink under, the world where nothing's as it should be, the way it ought to be for Orozkul according to his virtues and his position.

Giving in wholly to his anger, Orozkul led the horse through the bushes straight to a sharp drop. Let Efficacious Momun jig around the log if he could. And let him try not to keep control of the log. "I'll crack the old fool in half and that's that," Orozkul decided.

At any other time, he would never have dared to take a chance with a log in tow on such a dangerous incline. But he'd gone berserk. And Momun had no time to stop him, but only to utter a cry—"Where are you headed? *Where? Stop!*"— when the log spun in its chain and charged downwards, trampling down the bushes. It was a damp and heavy log. Momun tried to get his lever beneath it to arrest its downward motion, but the blow was so powerful that it knocked the lever clean from the old man's hands.

All this happened in an instant. The horse fell and was dragged down the slope on its side. In falling, the animal struck down Orozkul. He clutched convulsively at the bushes as he rolled. Just at that moment, some kind of horned animals started in fear within the thick foliage. Leaping high and powerfully, they took shelter in a grove of birch trees.

"Marals, marals!" cried grandfather Momun, beside himself with fear and joy. And then fell silent, as if not believing his own eyes.

Suddenly, everything grew hushed in the mountains. The jackdaws dispersed all at once. Having crushed strong young birch trees in its path, the log was caught by something on the slope. Entangled in its harness, the horse struggled to its feet by itself.

In tatters, Orozkul crawled to one side. Momun hurried to help his son-in-law.

"Oh sacred Mother Horned-Deer. She's the one who saved us! Did you see them? They're the children of Horned Deer-Mother. Our mother's returned. You saw yourself!"

Still not quite believing that the danger had passed, Orozkul brushed himself off, grim and flushed with shame.

"Stop babbling, you old fogey. That's enough. Get the horse there out of its traces."

Momun climbed down dutifully to disentangle the horse.

"Oh, wondrous Mother Horned-Deer!" Momun continued mumbling in joy. "The marals have returned to our forests. Our Horned Mother hasn't forgotten us! She's forgiven us our transgressions . . ."

"You're still twaddling?" snapped Orozkul. He had recovered from his fright, and as before, spite gnawed at his heart. "Blathering your fairy-tales? You're off your own head so you think other people will believe your goofy fables."

"I saw them with my own eyes. They were marals," said grandfather Momun, not giving in. "Didn't you see them, my son? You saw them yourself."

"So I saw something, so what? Kind of flashing by, three of them . . ."

"That's it — three. I thought so too."

"Well, what of it? What's so great about marals? A man's almost had his neck broken right here. What's there to be jolly about? And if they were marals, it only means they came through the pass. On the other side of the mountain — back over there, in Kazakhstan—they say some marals are still around. There's a big preserve there too. Maybe they're marals from that preserve. So they wandered over here—so what? What's it to us? Kazakhstan's none of our business."

"Maybe they'll like it here," mused grandfather Momun. "If they'd only stay . . ."

"C'mon, enough of that," Orozkul cut him short. "Let's get going! . . ."

They still had a long descent in front of them with the log, and then had to get it across the river, also by towing it in harness. That too was a hard job. And if they succeeded in ferrying the log safely across the river, they still had to drag it up the little hillock where it would be loaded onto the lorry.

Damn, all this work!

Orozkul felt utterly unlucky and unhappy. All around him, everything seemed unfair. The mountains felt nothing, cared for nothing and complained about nothing: they just stood there for the sake of standing. The forests were succumbing to autumn, after which they'd succumb to winter, which was never a hardship for them. Even the jackdaws flew around free and screeched themselves sick if they wanted to. Marals—if they really were marals—came through the pass and would roam the forest, how and where they wanted. In cities, people strolled happy-go-lucky along asphalt streets, rode in taxis, treated themselves to restaurants and had all the fun they wanted. And fate had pitched him into these mountains, he was ill-starred . . . Even this Efficacious Momun, his good-for-nothing father-in-law—even he was luckier because he believed in fairy-tales. A stupid man. Stupid people were always satisfied with life.

But Orozkul hated his life. It didn't become him. It was a life for people like Efficacious Momun. What did he need for himself, that Momun? As long as he lived he'd break his back day after day without a breather. In his whole life, he never had anyone under him, and he knuckled down to everybody, even his old lady—he didn't even cross her. A fairy-tale can make that kind of wretch happy. He sees some marals in the forest and it reduces him to tears, as if he'd met his blood brothers who he'd been searching for all over the world for a hundred years.

Ekh, what's the use of talking about it? . . .

Finally they came to the last ridge, from which the long, steep descent to the river began. They stopped for a rest.

Across the river, something was smoking in the yard of the cordon near Orozkul's house. You could guess by the smoke: it was the samovar. So his wife was already waiting for him. But Orozkul felt no better for this. He gulped his breath through his mouth, unable to get enough air. His chest ached and heartbeat drummed in his head like an echo. Sweat from his forehead stung his eyes. And his empty-bellied wife was waiting for him at home. Phoo, she was heating the samovar, hoping to play up to him . . . Suddenly he felt a sharp yearning to speed up and kick that pot-bellied samovar—kick it to hell. Then fall on his wife and beat her. Beat her to a pulp—to death. He savoured this in his mind's eye, hearing his wife screaming and cursing her miserable fate. "Let her scream," he thought. "Just let her. Everything's rotten for me—why should she have it good?"

Momun interrupted his thoughts.

"And I forgot, my son," he suddenly remembered, hurriedly approaching Orozkul, "I've got to go to school now, to fetch the little fellow. Classes are over already."

"What of it?" pronounced Orozkul with assertive calmness. "What are you suggesting?"

"Don't be angry, my son. Let's leave the log here. Get down off the mountain. You have dinner at home. Meanwhile, I'll gallop over to the school. Fetch the boy. We'll come back up and take care of the log."

"Did it take you a long time to think that up, you old fogey?" taunted Orozkul.

"But don't you see? The boy—he'll cry."

"So what?" raged Orozkul. At last he'd found something for which he could light into the old man well and truly. Orozkul had been searching all day for something to find fault with; now Momun himself had given him his chance. "He's going to cry, and that means we're going to drop our job? You pulled one over on me in the morning—you had to get him to school. All right, you delivered him. Now you're going to bring him back? And what am I supposed to do? You think we're playing games here?"

"Don't, my son," Momun appealed. "Not on a day like today. It doesn't matter about me, but the little fellow will be waiting. Will be crying—on a day like today."

"What? On what kind of day? What's so special about today?"

"The marals have returned. On a day like today, why start..."

Orozkul was not only taken aback but even fell silent with amazement. He'd already forgotten about those marals or whatever it was that had flashed by in the form of quick, leaping shadows while he was rolling around in the thorny bushes, his heart in his boots with fear. Any second he could have been ironed flat by the uncontrollable log. He couldn't care less about marals—or the old man's prattle.

"Who do you take me for?" he said in a low and furious voice, breathing into the old man's face. "Too bad you don't have a beard. Or I'd yank it, so you'd stop believing that other people are stupider than yourself. Who the hell cares about your goddam marals! That's all I need—to start worrying about them. Don't try to hoodwink me with your fables. Let's go, get back to that log. And don't you open your trap until we get across the river. I don't give a damn who goes to school or who's crying over there. Enough of this, let's get going..."

As always, Momun submitted. Realising that he wouldn't shake off Orozkul until the log was delivered to its destination, he worked away in silence and desperation. He did not breathe another word, although he was deep in anguish. His grandson was waiting for him outside the school; all the other boys had scampered home and he alone, his bereaved grandson, was waiting there for his grandfather, his eyes fixed on the road.

The old man pictured the scene: the whole class of children clattering out of school together and starting their dash for home. Their appetites had been well sharpened. Once on the street, they would catch the smell of the food being prepared for them, and run to the windows of their houses with excitement and delight. Their mothers would be waiting. Each one with a smile that made her child giddy with happiness. Through thick and thin, a mother always managed enough strength to smile to her child. Even when she raised her voice—"And your hands? Who's going to wash your hands?"—even then, the same smile was hidden in her eyes.

Since he'd started school, the hands of Momun's grandson were always smeared with ink. But grandfather was even pleased by this: it meant that the little fellow was busy with something meaningful. And now his grandson was standing there on the road, his inky hands clutching the beloved briefcase bought that summer. He was surely tired of waiting. By now he was anxious. He'd be keeping his eyes and ears peeled for his grandfather to appear on his horse atop the hill. Hadn't he always come on time before? When the lad came out of school grandfather would be waiting for him near by, already dismounted. All the other pupils dispersed to make their way home, and his grandson would run to his grandfather. "There's grandad," the boy would say to the briefcase, "let's dash." Running up to his grandfather, he would then hesitate in embarrassment. If no one was near by, he'd throw himself into grandfather's arms, hug him and thrust his face into his stomach, inhaling the familiar smell of old clothes and dry summer hay. At that time, grandfather was transporting cartloads of hay from the far bank; you couldn't reach it through the thick snow in winter, and it was better to bring the hay over during the autumn. Long after this, Momun went about permeated with the bitterish scent of hay pollen.

Grandfather would seat the lad behind him on the horse's rump and they'd ride home, sometimes at an easy trot, other times at a walk; sometimes silent, other times discussing one thing or another— and arrive home without noticing it.

Through a saddle-like hollow between two hills, they rode down to their homestead in the San-Tash canyon.

The lad's intense enthusiasm for school irritated old grandma. He'd barely wake up in the morning before he dressed with great speed and rearranged his books and notebooks in his briefcase. Old grandma was angered by his keeping the briefcase by his side through the night.

"What's this gluing yourself to that rotten briefcase? All it needs is to become your wife—it'd save us from bride-money..."

The lad took no notice of old grandma's comments; indeed, didn't quite understand what she was talking about. His principal concern was not to be late for school. He rushed out into the yard to hurry grandfather along. And calmed down only when the school was in sight.

Once they were late nevertheless. The week before, Momun crossed to the opposite bank on horseback at the crack of dawn. He'd decided to get in one load of hay in the morning. It would have worked, but the load came undone on the way and the hay spilled off. He had to pitchfork all of it in place again and harness the horse to the load. The hastily packed hay spilled off the load again at the water's edge.

His grandson was already waiting on the opposite bank. He stood on a pock-marked rock, swinging the briefcase and shouting something and calling. The old man tried to hurry and the ropes became impossibly tangled, tightening into knots. And the little fellow kept up his calling; the old man knew that he was already crying. Then he dropped everything —the ropes, the hay itself—mounted his horse and hurried across the ford to his grandson. More time passed before he got across: you can't gallop across the ford because of the volume of water and strength of the current. It wasn't fiercely dangerous in autumn, but in summer it could sweep a horse off its feet, spelling the end of the rider. When Momun made his way across the river at last and rode up to his grandson, the boy was already shaking with sobs. He wouldn't look at his grandfather, but only cry and repeat, "I'm late, late for school."

The old man leaned over from the saddle, picked up the boy, seated him, and galloped off. Had the school been near by, the little tyke would have run there himself. As it was, he didn't stop crying during the entire trip and the old man could find no way to soothe him. In this state, howling dismally, he delivered him to school. Class had already begun. He took him directly into the classroom.

Momun apologised to the teacher at great length, promising that it would never happen again. But more than anything, the old man was shaken by his grandson's crying and the suffering he felt in being late. "God grant that school always has that kind of pull for you," thought grandfather. "Still, why did the little fellow cry so? It can only mean that he bears some pain in his heart, some inner, unexpressed hurt..."

And now, scurrying alongside the log, running from one end to another, pushing and poking beneath it with the lever so that it wouldn't get stuck anywhere and slide more quickly down the mountain, Momun kept thinking: how was he making out there, his grandson?

Orozkul, by contrast, was in no hurry. He was leading the horse. Nor was it a place for any great hurrying: the descent was long and steep, forcing them to take the slope obliquely. But couldn't he really have complied with his request to leave the log here temporarily and return to fetch it later? Ekh, had he had the strength, he would have hoisted the log to his shoulders, marched across the river, and tossed it on the spot where the lorry would load it. Here, take your log and leave us alone. And he, Momun, would set out for his grandson.

But what chance was there for this? They still had to get down to the bank and across the little beach of river stones, and from there drag the log to the opposite side with the horse's help. And the horse was already worn out — how he'd tramped through the mountains, first up and then down... It would be still tolerable if everything worked out — but what if the log became stuck on the rocks in the middle of the river? Or if the horse stumbled and fell?

When they started across the water, grandfather Momun began imploring. "Help us, Horned Deer-Mother. Don't let the log get stuck, don't let the horse fall." Removing his boots and slinging them over his shoulder, rolling up his trousers above the knees, gripping the lever in his hand, grandfather Momun hurried after the floating log. They dragged the log sideways against the current. The water was as clean and transparent as it was cold. Autumn water.

The old man bore up: I don't mind, my feet won't fall off. Anything to get the log across as quickly as possible. But the log became stuck nevertheless, as if bad luck had willed it. It came to rest on a rock where the rapids were strongest. In such cases, you had to give the horse a bit of a rest and then to urge him on properly; one good jerk could free the log from the rock. But seated in the saddle, Orozkul mercilessly lashed the already weakened, fatigued horse. The horse went down low on its hind legs and kept slipping and stumbling, but the log didn't budge. The old man's legs were frozen and his eyes began to go cloudy. His head whirled. The precipice, forest atop the precipice, and clouds in the sky were tilting and falling into the river, where they floated down the swift current and returned again. Momun was on the verge of fainting. The damn log! Had it been dry, had it spent its time in the sun, it would have been a different story: dry timber floats by itself, the only problem is to keep it from drifting away. But this one had just been sawed down, and the portage across the river followed immediately. Who works that way? But that's how it had turned out. Shady business always comes to a bad end. Orozkul would never agree to leaving the log to dry out: the inspectors might drop in on a surprise visit and write up a report about the felling of valuable trees in a forest preserve. Since they'd cut it down, he had to get the log off the mountain and out of sight as quickly as possible.

Orozkul kicked the horse with the heels of his boots and lashed him about the head with his whip. He cursed and shouted at the old man as if he, Momun, were the cause of everything. But the log not only didn't respond, but stuck more and more fast to the rocks. The old man's patience gave out. For the first time in his entire life, he raised his voice in anger.

"Off that horse!" he commanded, approaching Orozkul with great resoluteness and pulling him out of the saddle. "Can't you see that the horse can't manage? Get off—and now!"

The astonished Orozkul obeyed in silence. With his boots still on, he jumped straight from the saddle into the water. From this moment, he seemed to go feeble-minded, losing control of himself and his senses.

"Now let's pull. Dig in and *pull*. Both together!" At Momun's command, they heaved on the lever, lifting the log from its place and freeing it from the trap of the rocks.

What intelligent animals horses are! Precisely at this moment, he gave a powerful jerk forward and, stumbling and slipping on the rocks, pulled his traces as taut as a string. But hardly had the log worked free and slid slightly forward when it became stuck again. The horse managed another forward jerk, lost its balance, fell into the water and floundered, entangling himself in his harness.

"The horse! Get the horse up!" ordered Momun, pushing Orozkul.

With great difficulty, they succeeded together in helping the horse find its feet. The horse trembled with cold and could hardly stand in the water.

"Unharness him!"

"What for?"

"Unharness him, I'm telling you. We're going to re-harness him. Take off his traces."

Again Orozkul silently obeyed. When the horse was unharnessed, Momun took it by the reins.

"Now let's get out of here," he said. "We'll return later. Let the horse get some rest."

"Hold on there!" snapped Orozkul, grabbing the reins from the old man's hands. It was as if he had awakened; suddenly he became himself again. "Who do you think you're fooling? You're not going anywhere. We're getting that log out of here right now. People are coming for it this evening. Get that harness on the horse and keep your mouth shut, understand?"

Momun turned away in silence and, hobbling on his frozen feet, waded across the ford to the bank.

"Where are you going, you codger? I said *where*?"

"You know where. To school. Grandson's been waiting since noon."

"Get yourself back here. I said get *back*!"

The old man paid no heed. Orozkul left the horse in the river and caught up with Momun in the pebbly shallow just before the bank. He grabbed him by a shoulder and spun him around.

They were now face to face.

With a sharp movement of his hand, Orozkul tore from Momun's shoulders the old canvas boots that had been hanging there, feet-down. He struck his father-in-law with them twice in the head and face—lashing out with all his might.

"Get back here," wheezed Orozkul, hurling the boots aside.

The old man trod to his boots and raised them from the wet sand. When he straightened up, blood appeared on his lips.

"You bastard!" said Momun, spitting out the blood and throwing his boots over his shoulder again.

This was uttered by Efficacious Momun, who had never contradicted anyone in his life. It was said by a pitiable little old man, blue with cold, with his old boots hanging from a shoulder and blood bubbling on his lips.

"Get back here."

Orozkul pulled him towards the river. But Momun broke away in a spurt of strength and silently moved off, not glancing around.

"All right, you old dunce, now you watch out," Orozkul shouted after him, shaking his fist. "I'll remember this!"

The old man did not look back. Climbing up to the path near 'lying camel', he sat down, pulled on his boots and walked quickly home. Stopping nowhere, he made his way straight to the stable. From there, he led out the grey horse Alabash, Orozkul's untouchable Sunday horse, whom no one dared to mount or even bridle so as not to spoil his gallop. Momun rode out of the yard bareback as if racing to a fire. When he galloped past the windows and the still-smoking samovar, the women who had dashed outside—Momun's old wife, his daughter Bekai and young Guljamal—realised immediately that something had happened to the old man. He'd never mounted Alabash or galloped like mad through the yard. They did not yet know that this was Efficacious Momun's rebellion. Nor what this rebellion would cost him in his old age.

Orozkul returned from the direction of the ford, leading the unharnessed horse by the reins. The horse was lame on a front leg. The women watched in silence as he approached the yard. They could not yet guess what was taking place inside Orozkul, or what he had in store for them on that day. What troubles, what terrors . . .

In soaked, squelching boots and wringing trousers, he approached them in a heavy, ponderous step, glancing sullenly at the women from under his brows. His wife Bekai got into a state.

"What is it, Orozkul? What happened? My goodness, you're wet through. Was the log washed away?"

"No," barked Orozkul, waving her off. "Here"—he gave the reins to Guljamal—"take the horse to the stable." He himself went to his front door. "Get into the house," he said to his wife. Old grandma wanted to go with them, but Orozkul would not let her set foot inside.

"Go on your way, you crone. You've got no business here. Go home and stay put."

"What's with you?" said old grandma resentfully. "What's going on? And the old man—what about him? What happened?"

"Ask him himself," Orozkul answered.

Inside, Bekai pulled the wet clothing from her husband, gave him a sheepskin coat, brought in the samovar and began to pour the tea into a drinking bowl.

"Don't bother," Orozkul refused with a gesture. "Give me something real to drink."

His wife fetched an unopened half-litre of vodka and poured some into a water glass.

"Fill it up," ordered Orozkul. Draining the glass in a single gulp, he wrapped himself in the coat, stretched himself out on a hunk of felt, and addressed his wife. "You're no wife to me and I'm not your husband. Get out now and don't set foot again in this house. Get moving before it's too late."

Bekai sighed, sat down on the bed and, swallowing her tears as she was accustomed, said softly:

"Again?"

"Again what?" Orozkul bellowed. "Get out of here!"

Bekai leapt from the house and, as always, began to wail through the entire yard, wringing her hands.

"Why, oh why was I born in this world, wretched as I am..."

Meanwhile, old Momun was galloping to his grandson on Alabash. Alabash was a fast horse, but Momun was more than two hours late nevertheless. He met his grandson on the way. The teacher herself was walking the lad home. The same teacher with the coarse chapped hands, in the same invariable coat which she was wearing for the fifth year running. The wearied woman looked gloomy. The lad himself, his tears long exhausted but with swollen eyes, walked beside her with his briefcase in his hands; he cut a miserable, humbled figure. The teacher scolded old Momun sternly. He stood before her, dismounted and with his head hanging.

"Don't bring the child to school," she said, "if you're not going to fetch him on time. Don't count on me—I've four of my own."

Once again Momun apologised; once again he promised that this would never happen again.

The teacher returned to Jelesai, and grandfather and his grandson set out for home.

Seated on the horse in front of his grandfather, the lad remained silent. And the old man didn't know what to say to him.

"Are you very hungry?" he asked.

"No, the teacher gave me some bread," the grandson answered.

"Why don't you say anything?"

The lad did not reply.

Momun smiled guiltily. "You're my touchy little one, aren't you?" He removed the old forester's cap from the lad, kissed him on the crown of the head, and replaced the cap.

The lad did not turn around.

They rode on this way, both depressed and taciturn. Momun did not give Alabash his head but held a tight rein: he did not want to jolt the boy on an unsaddled horse. Besides, there now seemed no point in hurrying.

The horse soon understood what was expected of him and ambled on in an easy trot. Snorts accompanied the clatter of his hoofs on the road. He was the kind of horse made to ride alone, singing quiet songs—just like that, for the joy of it. There's no end to things a man can sing about when he's alone with himself. About his unfulfilled dreams and long-past years, about how life was once, when he was in love ... A man likes to sigh over the old times, where something forever unobtainable resides. Exactly what it is, the man himself doesn't quite understand. But sometimes he wants to think about it—to feel something in his depths.

A good horse with good gait made a fine travelling companion.

Glancing at his grandson's close-cropped head, at his thin neck and protruding ears, old Momun thought that of his whole unlucky life, of all his work and efforts, cares and sorrows—of all this, what was left to him now was only this child, this still helpless creature. If only he'd live long enough to get him standing on his own feet. But if he were to be left alone, it would be hard for him. He was no more than a little corn-cob, but already had his own personality. If he were only a bit more easy-going, a bit less withdrawn ... Because people such as Orozkul will always hate and torment him, like wolves with a deer at bay ...

Now Momun remembered about the marals—those who had flashed by as swift, darting shadows just a while ago, and wrenched a cry of amazement and joy from his heart.

"Did you know, my son?" said grandfather Momun. "Marals have come to visit us."

The lad glanced over his shoulder.

"Really?"

"Really. I saw them myself. Three head."

"Where did they come from?"

"From the other side of the pass, I imagine. There's a forest preserve there too. Autumn feels like summer just now—the pass is open. So they came over to pay us a visit."

"And will they stay with us?"

"If they like it they will. If they're not disturbed, they'll even settle. There's more than enough forage. You could raise a thousand marals here ... In the old days, the time of Horned Deer-Mother, they lived here in multitudes ..."

Sensing that the lad was thawing out upon hearing this news and that his resentment was being forgotten, the old man began talking about ancient times and Horned Deer-Mother. Intrigued by his own story, it occurred to grandfather how easy it was to suddenly become happy and to bring happiness to others. If only life were always like that! Yes, just like this, like now, like this very moment. But life wasn't made this way. Together with happiness, grief was always stalking you, always ready to pounce into your life and heart: relentless, age-old grief, always trailing just behind you. Even at that moment, when he and his grandson were happy together, anxiety lurked side-by-side with joy in the old man's heart: how were things now with Orozkul? What was he cooking up; what would his reprisal be? What punishment was he scheming up for him, the old man, who had dared to disobey him? Because Orozkul would never simply let this pass. Otherwise he wouldn't be Orozkul.

And so as not to think of the misery awaiting his daughter and himself, Momun gave himself fully to describing the marals — their beauty, swiftness and nobility — for his grandson. As if he would be able to avert the inevitable.

Suspecting nothing of what awaited him at home, the lad was happy. His eyes flashed, his ears flushed. Could it actually be that the marals had returned? So it was all true! Grandfather said that Horned Deer-Mother had forgiven humans' transgressions against her and allowed her offspring to return to the Issik-Kul mountains. Grandfather said that three marals had come now to investigate things here. And if they liked what they saw, all marals would return again to their homeland.

"*Ata*," the boy interrupted his grandfather. "Maybe Horned Deer-Mother herself has come too? Maybe she wants to see how things are with us here, and then bring over her children, eh?"

"Maybe," uttered Momun uncertainly. He faltered. The old man felt uneasy: had he gone too far? Didn't the boy take his words too seriously? But grandfather Momun did not undertake to dissuade his grandson. Because it was already too late. "Who knows?" he said, shrugging his shoulders. "Maybe. Maybe Horned Deer-Mother herself has really come. Who knows . . ."

"But we can find out. *Ata*, let's go back to the place where you saw the marals," said the boy. "I want to see them too."

"But they don't stand still in one place."

"Still, we can follow their trail. We'll follow their trail for a long, long way. And as soon as we catch just the tiniest sight of them, we can come home. Then they'll understand that people aren't going to hurt them."

"What a child you are," grinned grandfather. "Let's get home first, then we'll think about it."

By now, they were approaching the cordon by the path behind the houses. The rear of a house is like a man seen from behind his back. All three houses gave no sign of what was taking place inside them. The yard was also empty and tranquil. A strong foreboding pinched Momun's heart. What could have happened here? Had Orozkul battered his poor Bekai? Got himself dead drunk? What else could have happened? Why was it so hushed, why was no one in the yard at that hour? "If everything's all right, I'll have to drag that infernal log from the river," thought Momun. "The devil with that Orozkul, it's better to have nothing to do with him. It's easier to do what he says and to hell with all this. You can't convince an ass that he's an ass."

Momun rode up to the stable.

"Down you go, we've arrived," he said to his grandson as if they'd come from far away. He tried not to show his alarm. But when the boy was about to run home with his briefcase, grandfather Momun stopped him. "Wait a minute. We'll go together."

He led Alabash into the stable and, taking the lad by the hand, walked towards his house.

"Look here," said grandfather to his grandson. "If I'm called all kind of names, don't be afraid and don't listen to anything. It doesn't concern you. Your job is to go to school."

But nothing of the kind took place. When they entered the house, old grandma only peered at Momun with a long, accusing glance and, pursing her lips, returned to her sewing. Grandfather did not speak to her either. Gloomy and guarded, he stood for a moment in the centre of the room. Then he took a large bowl of noodle soup from the stove and, fetching two spoons and some bread, sat down with his grandson to a late dinner.

They ate in silence and old grandma did not so much as glance in their direction. Anger stiffened her flabby brown face. The lad realised that something very bad had happened. But the old man and woman still said nothing.

Dread and anxiety so welled up in the boy that his food wouldn't go down. There is nothing worse than people keeping silent during a meal, while they concentrated on their own evil thoughts and schemed something hurtful. "Maybe it's our fault?" said the boy—in his thoughts—to the briefcase. The briefcase lay on the window-sill. The boy's heart crept along the floor, clambered up to the window-sill and snuggled close to the briefcase, with whom it began talking in whispers.

"Do you know anything about it? About why granddaddy's so sad? What's he done wrong? And why was he late today— why did he come on Alabash, and bareback? Because nothing like that's ever happened before. Maybe he saw the marals in the forest and that's why he was held up? . . . But what if there aren't any marals at all—if it's all untrue? What then? Why did he talk about them? Because Horned Deer-Mother will be very insulted if he tricked us . . ."

Finishing his dinner, grandfather Momun spoke quietly to the lad.

"You go out into the yard, I've got something to take care of. You can give me a hand. I'll be right out."

The lad left obediently. No sooner had he closed the door behind him when old grandma's voice rang out.

"Where are you going?"

"Out to haul over the log," answered Momun. "It's got stuck in the river a while ago."

"So you remembered all of a sudden," old grandma cried out. "Came to your senses. Go have a look at your daughter. Guljamal took her back to her place. Who needs her now, your unfertile fool? Go ahead, let her tell you who she is now. Her husband's tossed her out of the house like a mangy bitch."

"What can I say? If he's tossed her out, he's tossed her out," said Momun bitterly.

"Oh *you*. And who are you yourself? Your daughters don't know what to do with themselves and you think you're going to make a boss or something out of your grandson? Yeah, yeah, just wait. As if he's worth it; you're just begging for trouble. To top it off, you jump on Alabash and speed off. Take a look at you! If you only knew your place you'd understand who you're taking on. He'll wring your neck like a chicken. Since when did you start talking back to people? Since when did you become a hero? And don't have any ideas about taking your daughter in with us. I won't let her set foot in here . . ."

His head hanging, the lad made his way across the yard. Old grandma's cries were still resounding from inside the house when the door slammed and Momun hurried out. The old man started towards Seidakhmat's house, but Guljamal met him at the door.

"You'd better not just now," she said to Momun. "Later." Momun stopped, obviously perplexed. "She's crying, he gave her a terrible beating," she whispered. "He says that they're not going to live together now. And she curses you for it. She says her father's to blame for everything."

Momun did not answer. What could he say? Now even his own daughter didn't want to see him.

"And Orozkul's still home, drinking by himself," Guljamal recounted in whispers. "He's like a wild beast."

They lost themselves in thought. Guljamal sighed in compassion.

"If only our Seidakhmat comes back quickly. He's supposed to be here today. You could bring over the log together and at least take care of that."

"As if it was the log that matters," said Momun shaking his

head. He fell into thought again and, catching sight of his grandson near by, sent him away. "Go on and play a bit."

The lad left them. He went to the shed, uncovered his hidden binoculars and wiped them clean of dust. "Things aren't so good," he said sadly to the binoculars. "It seems that it's our fault, briefcase's and mine. If there was only another school somewhere—briefcase and I would go there for our classes. So that nobody would know about it. Only I'd feel sorry for grandfather; he'd be looking for us everywhere. And you, binoculars—who would you look at the white steamship with? You think I can't make myself into a fish? You'll see. And I'll swim out to the white steamship..."

The lad hid himself behind a haystack and began to look around through the binoculars. He did not look long, nor with any joy. On an ordinary day, he could have looked for hours: the mountains stood there in their autumnal splendour, covered with autumn forests. White snow lay up above; below were crimson flames.

The lad returned the binoculars to their place and as he left the shed saw his grandfather leading a horse, collared and harnessed, across the yard. He was setting out for the ford. The lad wanted to run to his grandfather but was halted by a sharp cry from Orozkul. In his undershirt, with his sheepskin coat on his shoulders, Orozkul leapt out of his house. His face was purple, like a cow's swollen udders.

"Hey you," he cried threateningly to Momun. "Where are you taking that horse? Take her back, damn you. We'll get the thing over without you. And don't you dare touch it. You're nothing around here now. I'm going to kick you off this cordon. Now clear off—I don't give a hoot where."

Grandfather grinned bitterly and led the horse back into the stable. Suddenly Momun had become very small and old. He shuffled on his soles and looked neither to one direction nor another.

Choked with hurt for his grandfather, the lad ran along the bank of the river so that no one would see him crying. Ahead, the trail became misted over, disappeared, and found itself again under his feet. Tears fell from his face as he ran. There they were, his favourite boulders along the bank: 'tank', 'wolf', 'saddle' and 'lying camel'. The lad said nothing to them; they understood nothing, just stood there, doing nothing but standing. The lad merely put his arms around 'lying camel's' hump and, leaning up against the ginger granite, sobbed violently, bitterly and inconsolably. He cried for a long time before the sobs gradually subsided and he calmed down.

At last he raised his head, wiped his eyes and, casting a glance out in front of him, grew rigid from head to toe.

Directly in front of him, on the opposite bank, stood three marals at the water. Real marals. Alive. They were drinking from the river and, it seemed, had already drunk their fill. The one with the largest and heaviest horns lowered his head to the water again, and while sipping seemed to examine his horns in the shallow back-current, as in a mirror. He was of a brownish colour, with a broad, powerful chest. When he tossed up his head, drops from his fair, hairy muzzle fell into the water. Pricking up his ears, the stag gazed at the lad.

But most intently of all, the boy was examined by a white round-flanked doe with a crown of fine branchy horns on her head. Although slightly smaller, her horns were extremely beautiful. She was exactly like Horned Deer-Mother. Her eyes were huge, clear and full. And she herself was like a stately mare who gave forth a new foal every year. Horned Deer-Mother stared steadily and calmly at the lad, as if trying to remember where she had seen this big-headed, big-eared shaver. Her eyes sparkled moistly and shined from afar. A light exhalation rose from her nostrils. Next to her, with his rump turned in this direction, a young, hornless fawn gnawed at a rose willow branch, caring about nothing else. He was plump, healthy and gay. Suddenly abandoning his gnawing at the branch, he gave a frisky jump, brushed against the doe with his shoulder and, jumping again several times, began to nuzzle himself against her. He rubbed his hornless head against Horned Deer-Mother's flank. But Horned Deer-Mother kept staring and staring at the lad.

Holding his breath, the lad emerged from behind the rock and, stretching out his hands before him as if in a dream, walked down to the bank and the water's edge. The marals betrayed no fear whatever, but observed him calmly from the opposite bank.

Between them flowed the swift, transluscent and greenish river, foaming up and surging over the obstructions of underwater rocks. If it were not for the river separating them, it seemed he could go to the marals and stroke them. They stood on a flat, clean pebbled beach, and behind them, at the end of the little strip of beach, blazed the shrubbery of the forest. Above this was a clayey precipice, above the precipice stood gold and crimson birches and aspens; and still higher was the huge forest itself and white snow on the rocky mountain ridges.

The lad shut his eyes and opened them again. The same scene lay before him, but the red-leaved foliage was now slightly closer, together with the same fairy-tale marals.

But now they turned around and walked Indian file across the beach and into the forest. The largest maral went first, the hornless calf was in the centre, and Horned Deer-Mother took up the rear. Turning around, she looked once more at the lad. The marals entered the thick foliage and made their way through the small trees. Auburn branches swung over them and red leaves drifted down upon their smooth, resilient backs.

Then they went off towards the higher ground along the trail, climbing up to the precipice, where they stopped. And again the lad imagined that the marals gazed at him. The large maral stretched his neck and, tossing his horns upward onto his back, thundered like a trumpet: "Ba-o, ba-o!" His cry rumbled over the precipice and the river in a protracted echo: "A-o, a-o!"

It was only at this point that the lad recovered all his senses. He whipped around to dash home along the familiar trail as fast as his legs could carry him, running to the very limit of his being. He flashed across the yard and, flinging open the door with a bang, shouted from the threshold between his pants for breath.

"*Ata*. The marals have come. Marals! They're here!"

Grandfather Momun looked at him from the corner where he was sitting, mournful and silent. He said nothing, as if he did not understand what the boy was talking about.

"That's enough of your noise!" hissed old grandma. "If they came, they came. Don't bother us now."

The lad left quietly. The yard was completely empty. The autumn sun had already tumbled down behind Guard Mountain and the neighbouring ridge of bare, dusky mountains, lighting the chilling mountain wildwoods with a thick but unwarming glow. From there, this cool glow diffused into unstable reflections over the crests of the autumn mountains. The forests were covered with an evening haze.

The wind blew down from the snow. The lad shivered. He was feverish.

VI

He was feverish too when he got into bed. For a long time, he couldn't fall asleep. Black night already reigned in the yard. His head ached. But the boy said nothing. No one knew that he had fallen ill. He was forgotten.

And there was much to make him so.

Grandfather was wholly confused and did not know what to do with himself. He would go outside, come in again, sit down for a minute, sighing heavily and grieving; then stand up and wander out again. Old grandma growled spitefully at the old man and also tramped back and forth, going out into the yard from time to time and returning. Curt, indistinct voices of some kind sounded in the yard, someone's hurried steps and someone's cursing—apparently Orozkul was swearing again. Someone was sobbing . . .

The lad lay still, growing more and more tired of the voices and steps, of everything he heard in the house and the yard.

He shut his eyes and, soothing his own loneliness and forlornness, remembered what had happened today, what he wished to see. He stood on the bank of the great river. The river flowed so swiftly that you couldn't look at it for long because your head swam. The marals gazed at him from the other bank. All three marals which he'd seen towards evening now stood there again. And everything was repeated again. The same drops fell into the shallow back-current from the muzzle of the big stag when he tossed his head up from the water. And Horned Deer-Mother kept staring intently at the lad with her kind, understanding eyes, just as before. Her eyes were huge, dark and moist. The lad was utterly amazed that Horned Deer-Mother could sigh just like a person. Full of sadness and grief, like grandfather. Then they departed through the foliage of the lower forest. Auburn branches swung over them and red leaves drifted down upon their smooth, resilient backs. They climbed up to the precipice and stopped there. The big maral stretched his neck and, tossing his horns upward onto his back, thundered like a trumpet: "Ba-o, ba-o!" Remembering how the big maral's cry had rumbled over the river in a long echo, the lad smiled to himself. After this, the marals took cover in the forest. But not wanting to lose them, the lad began to picture in his mind's eye what he wished to see.

And once again the big swift river flowed headlong before him. His head swam from the speed of its current. He made a leap, then flew across the river. Gently and smoothly, he crouched down not far from the marals, who continued to stand there on the pebble-bank. Horned Deer-Mother called him to her.

"Who's boy are you?"

The lad was silent; he was ashamed to say who his parents were.

"Grandfather and I love you very much, Horned Deer-Mother," he uttered. "We've been waiting for you a long, long time."

"And I know who you are. I know your grandfather too. He's a good man," said Horned Deer-Mother.

The lad filled with happiness, but didn't know how to thank her.

"If you want," he said suddenly, "I'll become a fish and swim down the river into the Issik-Kul to the white steamship."

He could do this. But Horned Deer-Mother didn't respond to the offer. Then the lad began to undress and, as in summer, went into the water, all huddled up and gripping the branch of the rose willow on the bank. However, the water turned out not to be icy but hot, burning and stifling. His eyes open, he swam under water, and myriads of golden grains of sand and tiny underwater stones spun around him like a buzzing swarm. He began to suffocate, but the hot stream kept pulling him further and further.

"Help, Horned Deer-Mother, help me," he shouted loudly. "I'm your son too, Horned Deer-Mother."

Horned Deer-Mother ran after him along the bank. She ran swiftly and the wind whistled in her horns.

The lad pushed away his blanket. He felt better immediately. He was wet with sweat, but remembering that in such cases grandfather wrapped him up even more warmly, he covered himself again more tightly. No one was in the house. The wick in the lamp had already burned down, making it burn dully. The lad wanted to get up for a drink, but sharp voices of some kind again resounded from the yard: somebody was shouting at someone, somebody was crying and someone was trying to offer comfort and calm. You could hear the commotion and the tramp of feet. Then two people tramped by right under the window, oohing and aahing as if one were dragging the other. The door swung open with a great noise and old grandma, breathing heavily in a white rage, literally shoved grandfather Momun into the house. The lad had never seen his grandfather so terrified. It seemed as if he had lost control of his senses. The old man's eyes wandered in confusion. Old grandma pushed him in the chest and made him sit down.

"Sit down, *sit*, you old fool. And don't poke your nose where it's not wanted. What is this, the first time they're at it? If you want things to work out, sit down and don't butt in. Do what I tell you, you hear me? Otherwise he'll hound us to death, you understand? Hound us off the face of the earth. And where are we supposed to go in our old age? Where?" With these words, old grandma slammed the door and hurried away again.

Once more it was quiet in the house. Only grandfather's hoarse, broken breathing could be heard. He sat on the step to the stove, hugging his head with trembling hands. Suddenly the old man fell to his knees and, raising up his arms, he groaned. Whom he appealed to was not known.

"Take me, receive me, wretched as I am. Only give her a child. I can't bear to look at her. Give her at least one, just a one and only — have pity on us . . ."

Crying and staggering, the old man rose and, clutching the walls, fumbled for the door. He stepped from the house, pulled the door partially shut after him and, behind the door, wept hollowly, squeezing his mouth shut.

The lad felt very bad. He was feverish again. Waves of heat and cold swept over him. He wanted to get up and go to grandfather, but his arms and legs did not obey and his head was filled with ache. Behind the door, the old man wept, and in the yard, drunken Orozkul was again raging while Aunt Bekai wailed desperately and the voice of Guljamal and old grandma tried to implore and persuade them both.

The lad left them for his imaginary world.

Once again he was on the bank of the swift river, and the same marals stood on the pebble-bank at the other side. The lad began to implore. "Horned Deer-Mother, bring Aunt Bekai a cradle on your horns. I beg you, bring them a cradle. Let them have a child." And he ran across the water to Horned Deer-Mother.

The water did not give way under his feet, but he came no closer to the other bank nevertheless, as if he were running in place. All the while, he kept begging and entreating Horned Deer-Mother. "Bring them a cradle on your horns. Make it so that our grandfather won't cry, so that Uncle Orozkul won't beat Aunt Bekai. Make them have a baby. I'll love them all, I'll love Uncle Orozkul too—only give him his child. Bring them a cradle on your horns . . ."

The boy seemed to hear a bell ringing in the distance—ringing more and more clearly. It was Horned Deer-Mother running through the mountains and carrying a small cradle on her horns, hooked under its arch—a birch *beshik* with a tiny bell. The cradle-bell jingled merrily. Horned Deer-Mother made great haste, and the little bell sounded closer and closer.

But what was this? The distant rumble of an engine joined the ringing of the little bell. A lorry was on the move somewhere. The vehicle's drone grew steadily stronger and more distinct while the little bell grew shy. Now its tinkling could be heard only irregularly, and it was finally lost in the engine's roar.

The lad heard the heavy lorry enter the yard, its metal parts rumbling against one another. All barks, the dog rushed into the yard. For a moment, the reflection of the headlights fluttered onto the window, then quickly went out. The engine too was switched off and the cab doors slammed shut. Talking among themselves, the men who'd arrived—three or so, judging by their voices—passed under the window behind which lay the lad.

"Seidakhmat's arrived," sounded Guljamal's joyful voice suddenly, and she could be heard hurrying to her husband. "We've been waiting for ages."

"Good evening," she was answered by strangers.

"How's everything here?" asked Seidakhmat.

"Not bad, we got along somehow. What took you so long?"

"And I'm lucky at that," Seidakhmat explained. "I made it to the state farm and waited forever for something moving in my direction. To Jelesai, at least. Just then these men were driving up to us for the timber . . . It's dark driving down that canyon. You know the road yourself . . ."

"Where's Orozkul?" asked one of the strangers. "At home?"

"At home," Guljamal answered uncertainly. "He's a bit under the weather. But don't worry about a thing. You can spend the night with us—we've got room. C'mon."

They moved off, but stopped after several steps.

"Good evening, *Aksakal*. Good evening, *Baibiche*."*

The newcomers greeted grandfather Momun and old grandma—who must have been ashamed by the newcomers for they should have greeted them in the yard, as outsiders are meant to be met. Maybe Orozkul would also be ashamed. If only he didn't disgrace himself and the others.

The lad calmed down somewhat and, in general, felt a bit better. The ache in his head was less severe. He even considered whether he should get up and have a look at the lorry. What kind was it, a four- or six-wheeler? New or old? And what kind of trailer did it have? Once last spring a real army lorry visited them on the cordon—it had tall wheels and a snub nose, as if somebody had cut off its snout. Its young driver, a soldier, let the lad sit in the cab—that was wonderful! And an officer with golden shoulder-straps went into the forest with Orozkul. What was it all about? Nothing like that had ever happened before.

"What's this about—are you chasing down a spy?" the lad asked the soldier. He grinned.

"Yeah, we're hunting a spy."

"We haven't had a single spy come our way so far," the lad breathed sadly.

The soldier burst out laughing.

* *Aksakal* and *Baibiche*: terms of respect for elderly men and women.

"What do you need a spy for?"

"I'd chase after him and catch him."

"My my, you're a nimble little fellow. But you're still small, you'd better grow up first."

While the officer with the golden shoulder-straps tramped in the forest with Orozkul, the lad and the driver warmed to their conversation.

"I love all lorries and all drivers," said the lad.

"And why is that?" the soldier asked.

"Lorries are good—strong and fast. Then they smell good, of petrol. And drivers: they're all young and all children of Horned Deer-Mother."

"What? What's that?" The soldier did not understand. "Who's that horned mother?"

"You really don't know?"

"No. I never heard of such a marvel."

"Then where do you come from?"

"I'm from Karaganda—a Cossack. I studied in a mining school."

"No, I mean whose son are you?"

"My father's. And mother's."

"And whose are they?"

"Also their fathers' and mothers'."

"And they?"

"Listen, you can keep on asking that forever."

"I'm the son of Horned Deer-Mother's sons."

"Who told you that?"

"Grandfather."

"Something's a bit funny somewhere," said the soldier shaking his head doubtfully.

He was intrigued by this large-headed boy with the protruding ears, the son of Horned Deer-Mother's sons. However the soldier was somewhat embarrassed when it was revealed that he not only didn't know where his clan had begun, but didn't even know the obligatory seven generations in his family tree. The soldier knew only his father, grandfather and great-grandfather. And beyond that?

"Didn't they teach you to remember the names of your seven ancestors?" the boy asked.

"No, they didn't. And what for? So I don't know—nothing's come of it. I've managed to live without it."

"Grandfather said that if people don't remember their fathers, they'll turn bad."

"Who'll turn bad? People?"

"Yes."

"Why?"

"Grandfather says that if this happens, nobody will be ashamed of the bad things they do. Because their children and their children's children won't remember him. And nobody will do good things. Because all the same, his children won't know about them."

"That's some grandfather you have," said the soldier with genuine wonder. "A very interesting grandfather. Only he stuffs your head with all kinds of rubbish. You're a big-headed fellow, after all—and you've got ears on you like our radar on the firing range. Don't you listen to him. We're marching to Communism, we're flying in space—and what's he teaching you? He ought to sit in on our political instruction sessions, we'd wisen him up in a wink. And you, you'll grow up some day, learn how things are—and see that you clear away from your grandfather. He's an ignorant one, backward."

"No, I'll never leave grandfather," the boy objected. "He's a good man."

"Okay, that's all right for now. You'll understand later."

Now, straining to hear the voices, the lad remembered the army lorry and how he wasn't able to make the soldier understand why local drivers, at least the ones he knew, were considered sons of Horned Deer-Mother.

The lad had told him the truth. There'd been nothing fabricated in his words. Last year, precisely at this time of autumn—or, it seemed, a bit later—the state farm's lorries drove up into the mountains to fetch the hay. They didn't come past the cordon, but just before reaching it, turned down the road into the Archa hollow. Then they drove up to where the hay had been mowed during the summer, so as to deliver it to the state farm in the autumn. Hearing a roar of engines like never before on Guard Mountain, the lad ran down to the fork. So many lorries all together! One after another—a whole column. He counted something like fifteen.

The weather was just about to break, any day now heavy snow would fall—and then 'goodbye hay until next year'. In this region, if you didn't get in the hay on time, you might as well forget about it. You couldn't drive through later. Evidently they'd dawdled with various jobs on the state farm and now that time was pressing, decided to bring in the waiting hay with all the lorries in one go. But it didn't work out...

However the lad knew nothing of this—and, actually, what business was it of his? Full of excitement and happiness, he simply ran towards each lorry, raced alongside it briefly, then ran towards the next one. The lorries rolled on, all of them new, with handsome cabs and wide windscreens. Young *dzhigits* sat in the cabs, sometimes two to a cab, all beardless and splendid specimens. The pairs had come to pack and load the hay. To the lad, they all seemed handsome, gallant and gay.

And generally speaking, he wasn't mistaken; that's the way it actually was. The young men's lorries were in good condition and travelled fast, passing the slope from Guard Mountain along the hard, rocky road. The young drivers were in a fine mood; the weather wasn't bad and on top of everything, a large-headed, large-eared whelp of a boy had appeared out of nowhere to run towards every lorry, bubbling over with wild delight. How could they keep from grinning at him and tossing him a wave—or sending him a little joking threat to make him even happier and more mischievous...

The very last lorry even stopped. A young fellow in army clothes—a field-jacket without its shoulder-straps and in an ordinary cap instead of a uniform one—peered out of the cab. He was the driver.

"Hi there, what are you doing here, eh?" He winked amiably to the little shaver.

"Just like that," answered the lad, not without a trace of fluster.

"You're grandfather Momun's grandson?"

"Yes."

"I knew it. I'm a Buguan too, you know. And all these fellows—they're all Buguans. We hit the road for the hay. Nowadays Buguans don't know each other, we're all scattered around... Say hello to your grandfather. Tell him that you saw Kulubek—Chotbai's son Kulubek. Tell him Kulubek's come back from the army and he's a driver on the state farm now. Well, so long now." And as a farewell gift, he gave the lad some kind of extremely interesting army emblem which looked like a medal.

The lorry growled like a wildcat and tore away, catching up with its mates. The lad suddenly yearned deeply to go off with that friendly, dashing fellow in the field-jacket, his brother-Buguan. But the road had already emptied and he could do nothing better than return home. He returned a proud boy, however, and told his grandfather about the encounter. The emblem was pinned to his chest.

Towards evening of that same day, the San-Tash wind suddenly struck from up high on the mountain ridge which reached the sky. It whipped up into a tornado. Leaves whizzed into a column above the forest and, rising higher and higher towards the sky, whirled over the mountains with a rumble. In a flash, a tempest was swirling so that you couldn't open your eyes. Snow followed immediately. A white host burst forth upon the land, the forest swayed and the river seethed. And the snow poured down; the blizzard raged.

Somehow, they managed to drive in the cattle and take in a few things from the yard; somehow they were able to carry an extra supply of firewood into the house. After this, no one poked his nose outside the house. Not for anything in the world in such an early but fearful storm.

"What can it mean?" wondered a worried grandfather Momun as he kindled the stove. He kept listening to the whistle of the wind, now and then going to the window. Outside, a haze of swirling snow was quickly thickening.

"Sit down where you belong," grumbled old grandma. "What is this, the first time we've had it? 'What can it mean, oh what?'" she mimicked. "It means that winter's come."

"So suddenly, just like that? In one day..."

"And why not? I suppose you should have been asked about it. Winter felt like it, so she came."

The chimney howled. At first the lad felt frightened and the cold went right through him while he was helping his grandfather with the chores. But soon the wood caught fire and it became warm; the house smelled of hot resin and the smoke of pine, and the lad calmed down while warming his bones.

They had supper, then went to bed. Meanwhile, the snow kept rushing down outside in swirls and the wind blew ferociously.

"It's probably really scary in the forest," thought the lad listening to the sounds outside the window. He felt uneasy when the sounds of muffled voices suddenly issued forth— some kind of shouts. Someone was calling somebody else and someone was answering. At first the lad decided that it was his imagination. Who could possibly have come to the cordon in these conditions? But grandfather Momun and old grandma also pricked up their ears.

"Someone's there," said old grandma.

"Yes," answered the old man uncertainly. Then he began to worry—who could it be at that hour?—and started dressing himself hurriedly.

Old grandma also hurried. She got up and lit the lamps. Fearful of something, the lad, too, quickly put on his clothes. Meanwhile, the people approached the house—many voices and many feet. Crunching the fresh snow under their boots, the strangers thudded across the veranda and banged at the door.

"Open up, *Aksakal*. We're frozen."

"Who are you?"

"Friends."

Momun opened the door. Together with currents of cold, wind and snow, the same drivers who'd driven past during the day to the Archa plateau for hay burst into the house, plastered with snow. The lad recognized them immediately. Kulubek too, in his field-jacket—the one who'd given him the military emblem. They were helping one of their number, supporting him by the arms; he groaned and dragged his leg. The house flew into a flurry instantly.

"*Astapralla!**What's happened to you?" wailed grandfather Momun and old grandma in one voice.

"We'll explain later. More of our group are coming, about seven men. They can easily lose the road. Come on, sit you down over here. Twisted his leg," said Kulubek quickly, seating his groaning mate on the step leading to the stove.

"Where are they, your others?" asked grandfather Momun impatiently. "I'll go out there and lead them in. And you run over," he said to the lad. "Tell Seidakhmat to get himself here quickly with the torch, the electric one."

The lad dashed out of the house and choked in the storm. He remembered that terrible moment until the end of his life. A kind of shaggy, cold, shrieking monster grabbed him by the

* *Astapralla:* 'God save us' in Kirghizian.

throat and began to shake him. But he didn't flinch. He broke free of the clutching claws and ran to Seidakhmat's house, protecting his head with his hands.

His route took him only twenty or thirty steps in all, but it seemed to him that he ran a great distance through the storm, like a chieftain to the rescue of his warriors. His heart filled with valour and determination. To himself, he seemed mighty and invincible, and before he reached Seidakhmat's house, he'd had time to achieve breathtakingly heroic feats. He leapt across chasms from mountain to mountain, struck down legions of enemies with his sword, and saved people drowning in rivers and burning in fires. In a jet fighter with a red banner streaming in the wind, he chased after the shaggy black monster and evaded him through canyons and cliffs. His jet fighter raced like a bullet in pursuit of the monster. The lad pumped machine-gun fire at him and shouted, "Crush the fascists!" And in all of this, Horned Deer-Mother was present. She was proud of him. As the lad was approaching the door of Seidakhmat's house at last, Horned Deer-Mother spoke to him. "Now go save my sons, the young drivers."

"I'll save them, Horned Deer-Mother, I swear it to you," said the lad aloud, and banged at the door.

"Hurry up, Uncle Seidakhmat. Let's get started to save our people." He spat out these words in a way that made both Seidakhmat and Guljamal recoil in fright.

"Save who? What happened?"

"Grandfather said we should run back with the torch, the electric one. The drivers from the state farm have got lost."

"Idiot," Seidakhmat scolded him. "Why didn't you say so?" And he scrambled to get ready.

But this didn't offend the lad in the least. How could Seidakhmat have known what feats he'd achieved to reach the house, or what oaths he'd uttered? Neither was the lad greatly bothered when he learned that grandfather Momun had met the seven drivers just outside the cordon and escorted them home. Because it all might have turned out very differently! Danger seems slight when danger has passed... In short, these men too were found. Seidakhmat took them home. Even Orozkul took in about five drivers for the night—he too had to wake up. All the others crowded into grandfather Momun's house.

The blizzard in the mountains did not subside. The lad would run out onto the veranda and in a minute couldn't distinguish where right was and where left, where up and where down. The stormy night whirled and raved. Snow piled up to knee depth.

Only now, after all the drivers had been found and thawed themselves out, after they'd recovered from their fear and the cold, did grandfather Momun cautiously pump them to find out what had happened, although it was clear that the blizzard had caught them on the road. While the young men described their ordeal, the old man and old grandma sighed.

"Oi, oi, yow!" They marvelled over what had happened and, pressing their hands to their chests, thanked God.

"You're dressed so lightly, you boys," reproached old grandma, pouring some hot tea. "How can you think of coming to the mountains in such flimsy duds? You're still kids, just kids. Showing off all the time—you want to take after city-folk. What if you'd been lost right through until morning, God forbid? You'd have frozen solid, like icicles."

"Who knew something like this would happen?" answered Kulubek. "Why should we dress warmly? If the worst comes to the worst, our lorries can always be heated from inside. You can sit there like at home. Spin the wheel around for amusement. Look at the height they fly at in planes—these mountains are no more than little hills from up above. Forty degrees below zero outside, and inside people sit around in their shirts..."

The lad lay on a sheepskin among the drivers. He snuggled close to Kulubek and was all ears to the grown-ups' conversation. No one guessed that he was even glad that a blizzard like this had blown up suddenly, forcing these fine young fellows to seek shelter with them in the cordon. Secretly, he set his heart on the blizzard not dying down for many days, at least three or so. Then they could live with them. It was so good when they were there, so interesting. It turned out that grandfather knew them all—if not the young men themselves, their fathers and mothers.

"There you are," said grandfather to his grandson with a faint note of pride. "You've met up with your brother-Buguans. Now you know what kind of brothers you have. That kind right there. Oh today's *dzhigits* are strapping, all right. God grant them good health. I remember the winter of '42 when they drove us out to Magnitogorsk, down to the construction site..."

And grandfather fell to telling the story, well known to the lad, of how they, the labour-soldiers who'd been transported there from various corners of the country, were set out in a long, long line according to height. It turned out that the Kirghizians were almost all at the very end: they were stunted. A roll call was taken, after which they had a smoke break. Some rangy fellow, red-headed and sturdy, approached them and started talking loudly.

"And where did these kind come from? Manchurians?"

Among them was an old teacher who answered.

"We're Kirghizians. And when we fought with the Manchurians not far from here, there wasn't even a mention of Magnitogorsk.* We were about as tall as you are then. Now we'll finish this war and grow some again."

Grandfather reminisced about this ancient incident. Chuckling and pleased, he glanced again at his house guests.

---

* The city became important in the eighteenth century on the basis of ore and coal deposits near by.

"That teacher turned out to be right. When I'm in the city or on the road, I look around: we've become a tall, handsome people. Nothing like the old days..."

The young drivers smiled understandingly; the old man liked to produce whimsical talk.

"We're tall, all right," said one of them. "But a lorry crashed down a slope out there. And all of us together didn't have enough in us to..."

"What did you expect, loaded down with hay and in this kind of blizzard?" said grandfather Momun in justification. "Things like that happen. God willing, it'll all be put straight tomorrow. The main thing is that the wind lets up."

The young drivers told grandfather how they'd driven up to the Archa's highest hayfields. Three large ricks of mountain hay were waiting there, and they began to load up all three simultaneously. They packed the loads high, higher than a house, so that they had to let themselves down on ropes afterwards. They loaded lorry after lorry in this fashion. You couldn't see the cabs, only windscreens, bonnets and wheels. Once they'd made the trip, they wanted to get in the whole lot so they wouldn't have to return. They knew that any hay left over would have to remain there until the following year. They worked hard, fast and well. When a driver's lorry was ready, he pulled over to the side and helped load the next one. They had packed on almost all the hay; not more than two loads were left. They had a smoke, agreed as to who would lead whom on the return trip, and all drove off together in a column. Driving cautiously — almost groping their way — they descended from the mountain. Hay isn't a heavy load, but cumbersome and even dangerous, especially on narrow roads and sharp turns.

They drove on, not suspecting what lay in store for them ahead.

They descended from the plateau of the Archa, drove down

the straits of the canyon, and as they were leaving the canyon — it was nearing evening now — were met by the tornado and the snow.

"It made your spine all sweaty, what started up there," Kulubek recounted. "Darkness all at once and a wind that ripped the wheel out of your hands. You were scared that your lorry would topple over any second. And on top of this, the road's dangerous even in daylight..."

Holding his breath, the lad listened. He lay stock-still, not removing his shining eyes from Kulubek. Meanwhile, the same wind and snow about which they were talking raged outside the window. Many drivers and loaders were already asleep side by side on the floor, still in their boots. And now all they'd endured was once again experienced by this big-headed lad with the thin neck and protruding ears.

Within minutes, the road became invisible. Like blind men following their leader, the lorries clung to one another, blowing their horns continuously so that none would drop behind. The snow fell like a wall; the headlights were lost in it and the windscreen wipers couldn't cope with the ice on the glass. The drivers had to press on by leaning out of their cabs — but can that be called driving?

The snow kept falling and falling. The wheels began to skid. The column came to a stop before a sharp rise where the engines raced as if mad — but all in vain. By this time, the lorries couldn't force their way upwards. The drivers climbed down from their cabs and, calling to each other and rushing from lorry to lorry, gathered at the head of the column. What to do? It was impossible to build a fire. To wait in the cabs would be to burn up the remaining petrol, which even now was hardly enough to get them back to the state farm. And if they didn't heat the cabs, they could quite easily freeze. The young men were lost for a solution. All-powerful technology had been rendered powerless. What could they do? Someone suggested tossing down the hay from one of the lorries so that everyone could bury himself in it. But it was clear that the minute a load was undone, not a wisp of hay would be left: the blizzard would whip it away before you could blink your eyes. Meanwhile, the lorries were being snowed under even more completely and drifts were already piling up over the wheels. Now the young men lost their heads completely and began to go icy in the wind.

"And suddenly I remembered, *Aksakal*," said Kulubek to grandfather Momun, "that when we were driving up to the Archa I met this one over here, our young brother-Buguan." He nodded towards the lad and patted him affectionately on the head. "He was running around on the road out there. I stopped—of course I did—and said hello. We had a little talk, isn't that right? Why aren't you asleep?"

Smiling, the lad nodded his head. If only anyone knew how violently his heart was thumping from pride and joy. Kulubek himself was talking about him. The strongest, bravest and handsomest of the whole group. How he'd love to grow up like him!

Grandfather praised him too while shoving a log into the fire.

"That's the kind our boy is. He likes to listen to people's talk. Look at that, how he's drinking in every little thing."

"How I remembered him at that moment," continued Kulubek, "I myself don't know. So I told my mates—shouted, practically, because the wind drowned out everything. 'Let's go,' I said, 'let's try to make it to the cordon. Otherwise we'll be finished here.' 'But how?' the others shouted in my face. 'We can't get there on foot. And we can't abandon the lorries.' So I said to them: 'Let's push the lorries up onto the mountain, and from there the road runs downhill. We've only got to get to the San-Tash canyon,' I said, 'and from there we can make it on foot to our foresters because it's not far at all.'

The lads saw the point. Okay, they said, you take command. Well, since it'd worked out that way ... We started with the lead lorry. 'Up you go, Osmonali, climb into your cab!' Then all of us, to the very last man, heaved at the lorry with our shoulders. And moved off! At first we seemed to make some progress. Then we ran out of strength. And couldn't retreat, either. Then it seemed we weren't hauling a lorry but a whole mountain. What a load!—a rick on wheels. I only know that I shouted with everything I had. 'Let's go, let's go, let's go.' But I couldn't even hear myself. The wind, the snow—you couldn't see a thing. The lorry howled and cried like it was alive. It inched forward with its last ounce of strength. And we too. It felt like your heart would burst and fly away in little pieces. We felt giddy in the head."

"Oi, oi, oi," said grandfather Momun in distress. "What you had to cope with! But somehow, I suppose, Horned Deer-Mother herself came to the aid of her children. She saw to the rescue. If it weren't for her, who knows? ... Do you hear that? It's not calming down out there at all, everything's still whirling and storming."

The lad could hardly keep his eyes open. He forced himself to stay awake, but his lids fell shut again. Half asleep, listening to snatches of the conversation between the old man and Kulubek, he fused reality with his imaginary scenes. It seemed to him that he too was there, among the young drivers stranded by the blizzard in the mountains. Before his gaze stretched a twisting road leading up to the whitest of white snow-covered mountains. The storm burned his cheeks. His eyes stung. They were pushing a huge lorry upwards, as big as a house and filled with hay. They made their way up the road very very slowly. Then the lorry went no farther, but gave up and shuddered backwards. It was awful. Frightfully dark. The wind was terribly scalding. The lad shrivelled with fear, sensing that the lorry would break loose and crush them. But now Horned

Deer-Mother appeared from nowhere. She braced her horns against the lorry and began to help them push it upwards. "Let's go, let's go, let's go," shouted the lad. And the lorry moved—actually moved. They pushed it up to the mountain, from where it ran down on its own. Then they shoved up a second lorry and a third and many, many more—each time helped by Horned Deer-Mother. No one saw her. No one knew she was there, by their side. But the lad saw and knew. He noticed that every time it became unbearably hard, when their strength was exhausted and it had turned dangerous and frightening, Horned Deer-Mother ran up and helped them roll the lorry upwards with her horns. "Let's go, let's go, let's go," the lad joined in. And all the while, he was alongside Kulubek. Then Kulubek told him: "Get behind the wheel." The lad mounted the cab. The lorry shook and droned. The wheel spinned by itself in the lad's hands—freely, like a barrel hoop with which he'd played car when he was still a toddler. The lad felt ashamed that his wheel had turned out like that, toy-like. Suddenly the lorry began to careen and fall on its side, then rolled over with a crash and broke into pieces. The lad began to sob loudly. He was terribly ashamed. Ashamed to look into Kulubek's eyes.

"What's the matter with you? What's the trouble, eh?" Kulubek woke him.

The lad opened his eyes and felt a surge of happiness that it had all turned out to be a dream. Kulubek lifted him in his arms and hugged him.

"Were you dreaming? Did you get scared? What a hero you are." He kissed the lad with his chapped, windbitten lips. "Let's go, I'll put you to bed. It's time you were asleep."

He laid the lad down on a cushion on the floor among the sleeping drivers. And he himself lay down alongside, pulling the lad close to his side and covering him with a flap of his field-jacket.

Early in the morning, the lad was wakened by his grandfather.

"Wake up," said the old man quietly. "Get dressed warmly — you can give me a hand. Get up."

Outside the window, the darkness of early morning could be seen. In the house, the men were still sleeping side by side.

"Here, put on these felt boots," said grandfather Momun. Grandfather smelled of fresh hay, which meant he'd already fed the horses. The lad pulled on the felt boots and went out into the yard together with grandfather. The snow lay in great drifts but the wind had died down. Only ground currents ran close along the snow from time to time.

"It's cold," the lad shivered.

"That's nothing," mumbled the old man. "It seems to be clearing up. What a business! The first of the year, and it whipped up like that. Never mind, as long as nothing terrible happened."

They went into the sheep-shed where five of Momun's sheep were being kept. The old man groped for the lantern on a post and lit it. The sheep peered at them from a corner and wheezed.

"Take this, you can hold the light for me," said the old man to the lad, handing him the lantern. "We'll slaughter the black ewe. The house is full of guests. We've got to get some meat ready before they get up."

The lad saw to the lighting for grandfather. The wind still whistled in the cracks; it was still cold and dusky outside. First the old man tossed an armful of fresh hay at the doorway. He led the black ewe there, but before felling her and binding her legs, turned thoughtful and squatted on his haunches.

"Set the lantern down," he said to the lad. "And you sit down too." Stretching his palms out before him, he began to whisper. "O great ancient mother of ours, Horned Deer-Mother. I am delivering this black sheep to you as a sacrifice.

For rescuing our children in an hour of danger. For your white milk, with which you nourished our ancestors; for your kindness and your motherly gaze. Do not abandon us on our passes, our stormy river and our slippery trails. Do not ever abandon us on our land; we are your children. Amen!"

He drew his palms down across his face beseechingly from his forehead to his chin. The lad did the same. Then grandfather felled the sheep and bound her legs. He unsheathed his old Asian knife.

And the lad held the lantern for him.

The weather turned calm at last. Once or twice the sun peered, as if frightened, from gaps in the racing clouds. Signs of the previous stormy night lay everywhere: random drifts, crumpled bushes, young trees with boughs bent by the weight of the snow and old trees which had fallen. The forest beyond the river was silent, tranquil and somehow dispirited. And the river itself seemed to be running lower; augmented by snow, the banks had become steeper. The water's noises were quieter.

The sun remained unsteady, alternately appearing and disappearing. But nothing darkened or disquieted the lad's heart. The worries of the previous night were dismissed, the blizzard forgotten and the snow no annoyance—it even made life more amusing. He rushed here and there, leaving only a spray of snow visible. He was happy because the house was full of people and the young drivers had slept well, and now talked loudly and laughed. And because they ate the lamb cooked for them with gusto.

Meanwhile, the sun was returning to normal. It shone more clearly and for longer intervals. The clouds dispersed somewhat and it even became warmer. The unseasonable snow began to sink rapidly, especially on the roads and trails.

True, the lad began to feel anxious when the drivers and loaders made preparations to leave. They went out into the yard and said their goodbyes to their host, thanking him for their food and shelter. Grandfather Momun and Seidakhmat accompanied them on horses. Grandfather took along a stack of wood and Seidakhmat a large galvanised tank to heat water for the frozen motors.

They all started off from the yard.

"*Ata*, I want to go too," said the boy, running up to his grandfather. "Take me with you."

"You can see for yourself: I'm taking the firewood and Seidakhmat's taking the tank. Nobody has room for you. Anyway, why do you want to tramp out there? You'll tire yourself out walking in that snow."

Keenly hurt, the lad pouted. Then Kulubek took him along.

"Come on with us," he said, taking the lad's hand. "You can go back with your grandfather."

They set out towards the fork, to the point where the road descended from the Archa's hayfields. There was still a good deal of snow. It turned out to be not so easy to keep pace with the strong young men, and the lad began to feel tired.

"Come on there, get up on my shoulders," suggested Kulubek. He gripped the boy by the arm deftly, and nimbly lifted him up onto his shoulders. And carried him with such accustomed ease that one would have thought he did it every day.

"You do it fine, Kulubek," said the driver walking alongside.

"I carried my brothers and sisters all my life," boasted Kulubek. "Because I'm the eldest and there were six of us. Mother worked in the fields, and father too. Now my sisters already have children. I came home from the army unmarried and hadn't yet gone to work, and my sister—the eldest one—said, come on over and live with us, you're a smashing child nurse. No, no I said to her—that's enough. From now on, I'm going to carry my own children around."

They walked on in this way, talking of one thing and

another. Riding Kulubek's powerful shoulders, the lad felt happy and secure.

"If only I had a brother like this," he thought. "I wouldn't be afraid of anybody. Just let Orozkul try and shout at grandfather or lay a hand on anybody. One firm glance from Kulubek and he'd quiet down in a second."

It turned out that the lorries which had been left the previous night were about two kilometres above the fork. Snowbound, they looked like winter haystacks in a field. It seemed as if no one and nothing could budge them.

But they built a fire and heated some water. They started turning over one of the motors with a crank, and it came to life, coughed, and started. After this, the work went quickly. Each succeeding lorry was started by using a tow. Each running and warmed lorry then towed the one behind it in the column.

When all the lorries were working, they fixed up a double tow and lifted up the one which had run off the road at night. Everyone present helped drag it back onto the road. The lad too found a place for himself on the edge of things and lent a hand. He kept worrying that someone would say, "What are you doing here, getting under everybody's feet? Make tracks and get yourself out of here." But no one said these words and no one drove him off. Perhaps because it was Kulubek who'd allowed him to help. And he was the strongest of all; everyone respected him.

The drivers again said their goodbyes and the lorries started off. Slowly at first, but faster and faster. They stretched out like a caravan along the road among the snowy mountains. The sons of Horned Deer-Mother's sons drove off. They didn't know that on the strength of a child's imagination, Horned Deer-Mother ran, invisible, ahead of them on the road. With long, swift leaps, she bounded ahead of the column, protecting them against accidents and mishaps on the difficult route. From snowslides and avalanches, from blizzards and fog; and from other adversities which had caused the Kirghizians so many tragedies in their centuries of nomadic life. After all, hadn't grandfather asked this of Horned Deer-Mother when he'd delivered a black sheep to her in sacrifice at dawn?

They drove off. And the lad went with them in his imagination. He sat in the cab alongside Kulubek. "Uncle Kulubek," he told him. "Horned Deer-Mother's running ahead of us on the road." "Really?" "It's true. Honest. There she is."

"Well now, what are you all lost in thought about? What's the point of standing around like that?" Grandfather Momun brought him to himself. "Come on, climb on here, it's time to go home." He leaned over on his horse and lifted the boy up into the saddle. "Are you cold?" asked the old man, and wrapped the skirt of his coat tighter around him.

When this took place, the lad hadn't yet started school.

But now, occasionally waking from his arduous sleep, his thoughts were troubled. "How will I go to school tomorrow? Because I'm really sick, I feel very bad ..." Then he would drift off again. He dreamt that he was copying into his notebook words the teacher wrote on the blackboard. "*At. Ata. Taka.*"* He filled an entire notebook with the first-form characters, page after page. "*At. Ata. Taka. At. Ata. Taka.*" He grew tired, his eyes fluttered and it became extremely hot. The lad removed his covers, and as he lay uncovered and growing cold, various visions again appeared before his eyes. At times he'd swim as a fish in the ice-cold river, swim out to the white steamship—but could not reach it, no matter what he did. Or he'd find himself in a fierce blizzard. In a cold, foggy storm, lorries loaded with hay skidded on a steep road leading

---

* *At, ata, taka:* horse, father, horseshoe in Kirghizian.

up a mountain. The lorries sobbed like people and all skidded in place. Spinning madly, the wheels turned fire-red. The tyres burned, sending flames shooting up from the rubber. Bracing her horns against the body, Horned Deer-Mother thrust the lorry loaded with hay up the mountain. The lad helped her, straining with all his strength and drenched in hot sweat. And suddenly, the load of hay turned into a baby's cradle. "Let's run quickly now," Horned Deer-Mother told the lad. "We'll take the *beshik* to Aunt Bekai and Uncle Orozkul." They started running. The lad fell behind. But in the darkness ahead, the cradle's bell kept ringing and ringing, and the lad ran towards its call.

He awoke to the sounds of steps on the veranda and the squeaking of the door. Grandfather Momun and old grandma had returned, seemingly somewhat calmed. Apparently the driver's arrival at the cordon had forced Orozkul and Aunt Bekai to quiet down. But perhaps Orozkul had wearied of his drunkenness and fell asleep at last. Neither cries nor curses could be heard in the yard.

Near midnight, the moon rose over the mountains and hung like a misty disc over the highest icy peak. Fettered by eternal ice, the mountain towered in the murkiness, glistening like a spectre with rough facets. Around it lay the foothills, cliffs and black, motionless forests in total muteness; and at the very bottom, the river pulsed over the rocks with its sounds.

The moon's faltering light streamed through the window in oblique rays. The light bothered the lad. He tossed about and screwed up his eyes. He wanted to ask old grandma to put a curtain over the window—but didn't: old grandma was angry with grandfather.

"You're a fool," she whispered as she got into bed. "If you don't know how to behave yourself with people, you should at least keep your mouth shut. Better listen to others. You're in his hands. Your pay comes from him, piddling as it is. Still, it comes every month. And who are you without pay? An old geezer, and you still can't think straight."

The old man did not answer. Old grandma fell silent. Suddenly, she shouted: "If a man's pay is taken away he's no man any more. He's nobody."

Again the old man made no answer.

The lad couldn't fall asleep. His head hurt and thoughts tumbled. He thought of school and felt anxious. He hadn't yet missed a single day, and couldn't imagine what would happen if he weren't able to go to his school tomorrow in Jelesai. And the lad thought too that if Orozkul kicked grandfather out of his job, old grandma would make the old man's life impossible. What then would become of them?

Why did people act this way? Why were some wicked and others kind? Why were there happy people and unhappy ones? Why were there some whom everybody feared and some whom nobody did? Why did some have children and others none? Why could some people keep back other people's pay? Probably the best people were those who got the most pay. For here was grandfather, who got little—and everybody insulted him. Oh, how to make it so that old grandfather also got more pay? Maybe then Orozkul would begin to respect him.

These thoughts made the lad's head ache even worse. Again he remembered the marals which he'd seen towards evening at the ford across the river. How were they getting on there at night? Because they were all alone on the cold, rocky mountains, in the pitch-black, impenetrable forest. It was terribly, terribly frightening there. What if they were suddenly attacked by wolves? Then who'd bring Aunt Bekai a magic cradle on her horns?

He fell into a troubled sleep and while drifting off, pleaded with Horned Deer-Mother to bring a birch *beshik* for Orozkul and Aunt Bekai. "Please let him have children, please bring them children," he implored Horned Deer-Mother. Then he heard the distant tinkling of a little cradle-bell. Horned Deer-Mother was hurrying near, with a magic cradle hooked on her horns . . .

VII

THE LAD WOKE early in the morning from the touch of a hand. Grandfather's hand was cold from the outdoors. The lad involuntarily huddled himself up.

"Lie there, just lie still." Grandfather warmed his hands with his breath, then felt the lad's forehead and placed his palm on his chest and stomach. "Have you come down with something?" asked grandfather with distress. "You've got a fever. And I was wondering, what's he doing in bed? It's time for school."

"Right away, I'm getting up," said the lad lifting his head slightly. Everything whirled before his eyes and there was a buzzing in his ears.

"Don't you even dream of getting up." Grandfather settled the lad on the pillow. "Who's going to take you to school, sick like that? All right, let's see your tongue."

The lad tried to persist.

"The teacher will scold me. She's very cross when children skip school."

"She won't scold anybody. I'll tell her myself. Come on, let's see your tongue."

Grandfather carefully examined the lad's tongue and throat. For some time, he felt for his pulse: coarsened by hard work, grandfather's rough fingers by some miracle caught the heart's impulses in the lad's hot, sweaty wrist. Convinced of something, the old man uttered comfortingly.

"God is merciful. You've just got yourself a cold. The cold got into you. You lie in bed today and before you go to sleep, I'll rub your soles and chest with hot sheep fat. You'll sweat it out and, God willing, get up tomorrow morning like a wild donkey."

Remembering yesterday and what still awaited him, old man that he was, Momun grew gloomy. Sitting at his grandson's bedside, he sighed and fell into thought.

"Forget about it," he whispered with a sigh. "When did you get sick, then?" he addressed the lad. "Why didn't you say anything? Was it last evening, or when?"

"Yes, towards evening. When I saw the marals across the river. I ran back to you. Then I began to feel cold."

"Never mind," the old man said, for some reason with a guilty voice. "You lie there and I'll be off."

He stood up, but the lad stopped him.

"*Ata*, that was Horned Deer-Mother herself out there, wasn't it? The one that was white as milk. And with those eyes — they looked at you like a person's . . ."

"You're a funny little one," said old man Momun, smiling warily. "All right, let it be your way. Maybe it was her," he said hollowly. "Wondrous Deer-Mother, who knows. I reckon that . . ."

The old man did not finish. Old grandma appeared at the door. Hurrying in from the yard, she'd already wormed something out.

"You get yourself over there, old man," she began from the threshold. At this grandfather Momun immediately hung his head, turning pitiful and dejected. "They want to drag the log out of the river with a lorry," said old grandma. "So you get over there and do everything you're ordered ... Oh my God, the milk isn't even boiled," old grandma suddenly remembered and set about lighting the stove and clattering the dishes.

The old man frowned. He wanted to object to something, to say something. But old grandma wouldn't let him open his mouth.

"What are you staring at?" old grandma said in annoyance. "What's this pig-headed nonsense? We can't afford to be pig-headed, sorrow of my life. Who are you against them? Big men have come to see Orozkul, go have a look. And what a lorry they came in! You can load it up with ten logs and it'll still get them through the mountains. And Orozkul won't even look at us. No matter how I pleaded with him and lowered myself. He won't let your daughter set foot in the house. Your barren-belly is hanging around at Seidakhmat's. She's cried her eyes out—and curses you, her brainless father."

"That's enough." The old man lost his patience and, heading towards the door, said, "Give the little shaver some hot milk, he's sick, understand?"

"I'll give him the hot milk, I'll give it to him. And you get going for the love of God." Driving the old man out, she was still mumbling. "What on earth's come over him? He never crossed anybody, he was as meek as a lamb—then this all of a sudden. On top of everything he jumps on Orozkul's stallion, then gallops away on it. All this is because of you," she said shooting an evil glance in the lad's direction. "If only it'd been somebody worth-while to stir up a hornet's nest for."

She brought the lad some hot milk with yellow boiled butter. The milk burned his lips but old grandma insisted, forcing him.

"Drink it as hot as you can, don't be afraid to drink. Only hot stuff can drive out the cold."

The lad burned himself and tears appeared in his eyes. And old grandma suddenly grew kinder.

"All right cool yourself down a bit. Imagine that," she sighed, "he gets himself sick at a time like this."

For a long time now the lad had badly wanted to urinate. He got up, feeling a kind of strange, pleasant weakness throughout his body. But old grandma held him back.

"What's this, you want to piss?"

"Yes," the lad confessed.

"Wait a minute. I'll be right back."

She brought him a basin.

Turning aside awkwardly, the lad directed a stream into the basin, puzzling over the heat and yellowness of his urine.

He felt much better now. His head ached less.

The lad lay quietly in his bed, grateful to old grandma for her good turn. He decided that he must get well by morning and go to school without fail. He thought too of how he'd tell in school about the three marals who'd appeared in their forest. And that the white dam maral was Horned Deer-Mother herself, and with her was a calf, already big and strong, and with them was a strapping brownish maral with huge horns; he was very strong and protected Horned Deer-Mother and her young from wolves. And he thought of how he'd tell too that if the marals stayed with them and never went away, then Horned Deer-Mother would soon bring Uncle Orozkul's and Aunt Bekai's magic cradle.

In the morning, the marals made their way down to the water. They came down from the upper forest when the brief autumn sun had half risen above the mountain ridges. The higher the sun climbed, the lighter and warmer it became down below in the mountains. After the night's numbness, the forest came to life and filled with the stirrings of light and colour.

Threading their way through the trees, the marals moved unhurriedly, warming themselves in sunny clearings and nibbling at dewy leaves on branches. They were travelling in the same order—the stag in front, calf in the middle, and bulky-flanked dam, Horned Deer-Mother, at the rear—and descended along the same trail on which Orozkul and grandfather Momun had yesterday hauled the ill-fated pine log towards the river. Traces of the portage remained fresh on the black mountain soil: a ploughed furrow with tattered shreds of turf. This trail led to the ford where the log had been abandoned, stuck in the river's rapids.

The marals were heading here because it was convenient for watering. Orozkul, Seidakhmat and the two men who had come for the log were going there to see how best to drive up the lorry so as to hook on a steel cable and drag the log from the river. Grandfather Momun shambled uncertainly behind the others, hanging his head. He didn't know how to act after yesterday's brawl, how to conduct himself or what to do. Would Orozkul let him work? Would he drive him off, like yesterday when he'd wanted to pull out the log with the horse? What if he said: "And what are you doing here? Weren't you told that you're fired from your job?" What if he dressed him down in front of the others and sent him home? The old man was beset by doubts and walked as if to a place of torture—but kept on nevertheless. Old grandma followed behind. She came as if on her own business, seemingly out of curiosity. But in fact she was escorting the old man. She'd driven Efficacious Momun to a reconciliation with Orozkul, so that he would merit Orozkul's forgiveness.

Orozkul strode on with an air of importance and proprietorship. Puffing and panting, he looked severely all around him as he moved. And although his head ached from his binge, he was enjoying the satisfaction of revenge. Looking back, he saw grandfather Momun shuffling after him, like a devoted dog after a beating by his master. "This is nothing so far—you'll sing yet another tune for me. I won't even set eyes on you now. For me, you're empty space. More's coming. You'll fall at my feet at your own choice." Orozkul gloated, remembering how his wife had howled with a heart-rending cry at his feet the night before—when he had booted her and drove her out of the house with his kicks. "That's the way it's going to be. I'll send off the two men with the logs here and then I'll bring them together once more so they have a nice wrangle. Now she'll gouge out her father's eyes. She's gone wild, like a she-wolf," thought Orozkul during breaks in the conversation while pressing on with one of the men who'd arrived.

This man was called Koketai. He was a dark, hefty muzhik—a collective farm lock-keeper from the lake-land who had long cultivated a friendship with Orozkul. A dozen or so years ago, Koketai had built himself a house. Orozkul helped with the timber, selling him logs on the cheap for sawing up into planks. Then the muzhik married off his eldest son and built a house for the young couple. Again Orozkul supplied the timber. Now Koketai was setting up his younger son in a separate house and once more timber was needed for construction. And again his old friend Orozkul gave him a hand. Wasn't it terrible, how hard life was! You finished one thing and you thought, all right, now I'm going to live in peace. But then life thought up something new for you. And nowadays you were lost without people like Orozkul.

"God willing, we'll be inviting you to the house-warming soon," said Koketai to Orozkul. "Come on out to our place, we'll celebrate properly."

The latter puffed smugly and exhaled his cigarette smoke.

"Thanks. When I'm invited, I don't refuse. And if I'm not invited, I don't fish for it. If you ask me—right, I'll come. It won't be the first time I've enjoyed your hospitality. I was just thinking: shouldn't you wait till evening so you can drive out in the dark? The main thing is to get through the state farm unnoticed. Otherwise, if they spot you..."

"Yeah, that's true," wavered Koketai. "But it's a long time to wait until evening. We'll drive out on the quiet. There's no control point on the road, is there, to check us? If we bump into the police or somebody else by accident..."

"That's the whole thing," grumbled Orozkul, wincing from heartburn and his headache. "You can drive around on your errands for a hundred years and not meet one of those dogs. But you haul some logs once in a hundred years and get into a pretty pickle. It's always like that..."

They fell silent, each thinking his own thoughts. Orozkul was now deeply vexed that he'd had to abandon the log in the river yesterday. Otherwise it would have been ready; they'd have loaded it at night and sent the lorry out of sight at dawn ... Ekh, why did that lousy business have to turn up yesterday! All because of that old imbecile Momun—he decided to rebel, wanted to wriggle out of control, out of his subordination. Well, never mind! Whatever he tried, he won't get away with this so easily...

The marals were drinking when the group arrived at the opposite bank of the river. People are strange creatures—full of noise and commotion. Absorbed in their own talk and concerns, they didn't notice the animals opposite, just across the river.

The marals were in the red, morning-fresh bushes of the riverside woods, standing in water up to their ankles on the clear, pebbled bottom of the shallow along the bank. They drank in small gulps, unhurriedly and with breaks. The water was icy. The sun above shone more and more warmly and pleasantly. Satisfying their thirst, the marals took pleasure in the sun. The heavy dew which had gathered from the branches along the way evaporated on their backs. A slight mist arose from their fur. The morning was peaceful and blissful.

But still the people didn't notice the marals. One of them returned to the lorry while the others remained on the bank. Pricking their ears, the marals keenly caught the unaccustomed noises which reached them and stood stock-still, their skin quivering, when a lorry with a trailer appeared on the other bank, roaring and rumbling. The marals stirred and decided to move away. But when the lorry suddenly stopped, and ceased its roaring and droning, the animals lingered. Nevertheless, they cautiously began to move: the people on the other bank talked too loudly and moved about with too much bustle.

The marals trod slowly up the path into the thin woods along the river; their flanks and horns showing here and there among the bushes. Yet still the people did not notice them. Only when the marals began to cross the glade of dry sand to which the high water reaches did the people see them, as clearly as a hand before their faces. There they were, on the lilac sand, lit by the bright sun. The people froze in various poses, with open mouths.

"Look at that, look!" Seidakhmat cried first. "Deer. Where did they come from?"

"What are you shouting for, what's all that noise?" mouthed Orozkul casually. "What do you mean deer—they're marals. We already saw them yesterday. Where'd they come from? They just came, I suppose."

"Ai, ai, ai," said hefty Koketai with delight, and undid his throttling shirt collar out of excitement. "They're sleek, all right," he said admiringly. "Been feeding well..."

"And what a dam. Look at how she strides," the driver echoed him, his eyes goggling.

"Honest to God, like a two-year-old mare. I've never seen anything like it."

"And what a bull! Look at those horns on him," muttered Koketai, his pig-like eyes glistening with lust. "How does he carry them? And they're not afraid of a thing. Where could those kind come from, Orozkul?"

"They're from the preserve, I suppose," answered Orozkul importantly, with a full sense of his proprietor's eminence. "They came over through the pass, from the other side. They're not afraid of anything? Because they've never had a chance to be frightened—that's why they're not afraid."

"Ekh, if I only had a gun now," blurted Seidakhmat suddenly. "They'd fetch two hundredweight,* eh?"

Momun, who had been meekly standing to one side until now, could not restrain himself.

"What are you talking about, Seidakhmat?" he said in a low voice. "It's forbidden to hunt them."

Orozkul flung a sullen glance at the old man from the corner of his eye. "You still dare to show your tongue here," he thought with hatred. He wanted to smother him in curses so he'd drop dead on the spot, but restrained himself. After all, outsiders were present.

"Nobody asked for your lectures," he pronounced irritatedly, not glancing at Momun. "Hunting's forbidden over there where they live—on their own grounds. But they don't live over here with us. And we're not responsible for them—is that clear?" Orozkul glanced threateningly at the floundering old man.

"It's clear," answered Momun submissively and stepped aside, hanging his head. At this point, old grandma furtively jerked his sleeve again.

"If only you'd hold your tongue," she hissed reproachfully. Everyone dropped his eyes in shame.

Again they began following the animals, now moving away along the steep trail. The marals climbed up the precipice in Indian file. The brownish stag was in front, proudly carrying his powerful horns; then the hornless calf and Horned Deer-

* Two hundred kilos.

Mother, bringing up the rear. Against the background of the clean, clayey fault, the marals looked precise and graceful. Every step and every movement was visible.

"Ekh, what beauty," said the driver, giving in to his rapture. He was a lobster-eyed young man, seemingly very gentle. "What a shame I didn't bring my camera, there'd be some..."

"All right, enough of the beauty stuff," interrupted Orozkul in resentment. "And enough standing around. You can't fill your belly on beauty. Let's get going—back the lorry up to the bank, straight into the water so it's on the edge. And you, Seidakhmat, take off your boots," he commanded, revelling to himself in his power. "And you, too," he indicated to the driver. "Let's hook the cable to that log. And step on it—we've still got something else to take care of."

Seidakhmat set about pulling off his boots. They were slightly too small for him.

"What are you looking at?" old grandma shoved the old man imperceptibly. "Take off your boots too, and get into the water," she prompted in a spiteful whisper.

Grandfather Momun scurried to pull off Seidakhmat's boots, then quickly shed his own. Meanwhile, Orozkul and Koketai gave directions to the lorry.

"Keep coming—over here. Here, keep it rolling."

"Left a little. Left—that's it."

"A little more."

Hearing the unfamiliar noise of a lorry below, the marals quickened their pace on the trail. Glancing about in alarm, they leapt up to the precipice and hid themselves in the birch trees.

"Oi, they've disappeared," sputtered Koketai. He exclaimed this with regret, as if a prey had escaped from his hands.

"Don't worry, they can't go anywhere," said Orozkul boastingly, taking pleasure in having read Koketai's thoughts.

"You won't go until evening—you'll be my guest. God's willed it. I'll give you a proper treat." Giggling, he thumped his friend on the shoulder. Orozkul could be gay too.

"Well, if that's the way it is," agreed hefty Koketai, revealing mighty yellow teeth in his smile. "You're the boss and I'm your guest."

The lorry was already on the bank, its rear wheels in the water up to its axles. The driver would not risk going in deeper. Now they had to run the cable out to the log. If the cable was long enough it wouldn't be particularly difficult to pull the log free from the grip of the underwater rocks.

The steel cables were long and heavy. They had to drag them through the water to the log. The driver took off his boots unwillingly, examining the water with apprehension. He hadn't yet made his final decision: did it pay to get into the river in his boots, or would it be better without them? "Maybe it's better barefoot," he thought. "In any case, the water will pour over the tops. The depth out there—almost to the hips. And then to walk around all day in wet boots." But he also imagined how cold the water must be in the river today. It was this that grandfather Momun took advantage of.

"Don't bother with your boots, young fellow," he said scampering up to him. "Seidakhmat and I will go in alone."

"Oh you shouldn't, *Aksakal*," objected the embarrassed driver.

"You're our guest and we're at home here," grandfather Momun persuaded. "You just sit behind the wheel."

Then he and Seidakhmat pulled a stake through the steel cable's skein and dragged it out across the water, while Seidakhmat howled bloody murder.

"Aw, aw—it's ice, not water."

Orozkul and Koketai smiled condescendingly and encouraged him.

"Stick to it, don't lose heart. We'll find something to warm you up with."

But grandfather Momun didn't utter a sound—did not even feel the icy cold. Wedging his head into his shoulders to make himself less noticeable, he worked his way in bare feet along the slippery underwater rocks, praying to God about one thing only: that Orozkul would not send him back, drive him off, curse him in front of others—that he forgive him, silly miserable old man that he was.

But Orozkul said nothing, appearing not to notice Momun's zeal nor take him for a human being. In his heart, however, he triumphed in having crushed the rebellious old man. "Well, well," laughed Orozkul to himself insidiously. "He's crawled up and sprawled at my feet. If only I had a bigger roost to rule, it wouldn't be his kind who I'd be twisting around my finger. Not his sort I'd make crawl in the dust. If they'd give me at least a collective or state farm; oh yes, I'd put things in order there. They've got too loose with handling people now. Then they themselves complain: people don't respect the chairman, don't you see, people don't look up to the director. Some little field hand, and he talks to the bosses like an equal. Because they're fools they don't deserve to be in power. Is that the way to deal with people? We had the good days once upon a time: heads flew and nobody made a sound. On the contrary—people loved it even more, sang even more praises. That was the way all right! And now? The littlest nothing of the nothings, and he suddenly takes it into his head to cross you. All right, fine. Crawl to me—just crawl." Glancing in old man Momun's direction from time to time, Orozkul gloated.

Dragging himself through the icy water and cowering, the latter tugged the cable together with Seidakhmat and took satisfaction in the fact that Orozkul, so it seemed, had forgiven him. "Please forgive me, this old man, that it happened that way," he appealed to Orozkul mentally. "I lost control yesterday. Galloped to my grandson in school. Because he's all alone, you see—so I take pity on him. And today he didn't go to school at all. Came down with something. Forgive and forget—you're a part of the family too, remember. You think I don't want happiness for you and my daughter? If God granted it, if I heard the cry of a new-born of your wife, my daughter—you wouldn't get me to budge an inch, let God take my soul on the spot. I'd cry from happiness, I swear it. Only don't hurt my daughter, forgive me. And as for work, well, as long as I'm breathing, I'll work, all right. Do everything. Only tell me what you want..."

Standing off to the side on the bank, old grandma spoke to the old man with her gestures and entire appearance. "Keep trying, old man. You see, he's forgiven you. Do what I tell you and everything will work out."

The lad slept. He awoke but once, when a shot thundered out somewhere, then fell asleep again. Worn out by yesterday's sleeplessness and illness, he slept a deep and peaceful sleep. And in his sleep felt how pleasant it was to lie in bed, stretched out freely and unbothered by either fever or chill. He'd probably have slept through for a long time were it not for old grandma and Aunt Bekai. They tried to talk in undertones but made a clatter with the dishes, and the lad awoke.

"Hold on to this big cup here. And take the plate," said old grandma vivaciously in the hall. "And I'll take the sieve bucket. Oh my poor back. It's bushed. All this work we've done! But I'm so happy, thank God."

"Oi, don't talk about it, *Eneke*, I'm so happy too. Yesterday I was ready to die. If it weren't for Guljamal I'd have laid hands on myself."

"Don't talk like that," old grandma reasoned with her. "Did you take the pepper? Let's get moving. God himself sent this gift for your reconciliation. Let's go, let's get moving."

As they were leaving the house — already on the threshold — Aunt Bekai asked old grandma about the lad.

"Is he still sleeping then?"

"Let him sleep for a while. When it's ready, we'll bring him some nice hot broth."

The lad slept no more. Feet and voices could be heard from the yard. Aunt Bekai laughed, and Guljamal and old grandma answered her with laughter. Unfamiliar voices of some kind drifted to him too. "It's probably only the people who came last night," the lad decided. "That means they haven't left yet." Yet grandfather Momun couldn't be heard or seen anywhere. Where could he be? What was it he was so busy with?

Listening to the voices from outside, the lad waited for his grandfather. He wanted very much to talk with him about the marals he'd seen yesterday. Winter was coming soon, remember. They'd have to leave them a good supply of hay in the forest. They must have enough to eat. The best would be to tame them so that they didn't fear people at all, so they'd come straight across the river and right up to the yard. And here we could give them some treat that they liked best of all. I wonder, what do they like best of all? The little maral calf could be trained to follow him everywhere. That would be really wonderful. Maybe he'd even go to school with him?

The lad waited for his grandfather, but he didn't appear. Instead, Seidakhmat came in suddenly, extremely pleased about something and in a gay mood. Seidakhmat was unsteady and smiled to himself. And when he came nearer, the smell of alcohol cut into the lad's nostrils. He very much disliked this nasty, sharp smell which reminded him of Orozkul's petty tyranny and of his grandfather's and Aunt Bekai's sufferings. But in contrast to Orozkul, Seidakhmat grew kind and gay when he drank, and in general turned into a kind of harmless simpleton—although even when sober, he was not distinguished by his intelligence. In similar situations, roughly the following conversation would take place between him and grandfather Momun.

"What are you grinning at like an idiot, Seidakhmat? You're pickled too?"

"*Aksakal*, I love you so much. Honest, *Aksakal*, like my own father."

"Ekh, at your age ... Others race around in lorries out there, and you can't even cope with your own tongue. If I were your age, I'd at least be driving a tractor."

"*Aksakal*, in the army, the commanding officer told me that I'm no good at those things. On the other hand, I'm an infantryman, and without the infantry, you can't get anywhere."

"Infantry! You're a loafer, not an infantryman. And what a wife you have! God made an oversight. A hundred like you aren't worth one Guljamal."

"That's why we're here, *Aksakal*. I'm one and she's one."

"What's the use of talking with you? Strong as a bull, and brains ..." Grandfather Momun waved his hands in despair.

"Moo ... o," bellowed Seidakhmat in his direction, and laughed.

Then, stopping in the middle of the yard, he began to sing his queer song, which he'd learned God-knows-where.

> From the chestnut-chestnut mountains,
> I arrived on a chestnut colt
> Hey, chestnut dealer, open the door
> We'll drink some chestnut wine.
>
> From the brown-brown mountains,
> I arrived on a brown bull,
> Hey, brown dealer, open the door,
> We'll drink some brown wine ...

This could go on forever, since he arrived from the mountains on a camel, a cock, a mouse, a turtle, on anything that moved. The lad liked Seidakhmat drunk better than sober.

Which is why he greeted him with a smile when Seidakhmat came in tipsy.

"Aha!" exclaimed Seidakhmat in surprise. "And they told me you're sick. You're not a bit sick—why aren't you running around in the yard? This won't do." He fell into the lad's bed and, overwhelming him with alcoholic breath and the smell of raw, fresh-killed meat from his hands and clothing, began to tug at the lad and kiss him. Overgrown with coarse bristles, his cheeks burned the lad's face.

"Please that's enough, Uncle Seidakhmat," the lad begged. "Where's granddaddy, did you see him?"

"Your grandfather's there, I mean . . ." Seidakhmat whirled his arms vaguely in the air. "We're ah . . . we dragged the log out of the water. So we had a bit to drink to warm up. And now he's, I mean he's . . . now he's cooking the meat. Get up, why don't you? Come on, get dressed—let's go. What's all this? It's not fair. We're all out there, and you're alone here."

"Grandfather didn't give me permission to get up," said the lad.

"Oh cut it out, didn't give you permission. Let's go have a look. This doesn't happen every day. There's a big feast today. A full bowl, a full spoon, a full mouth. Come on, get up!"

He began to dress the lad with drunken awkwardness.

"I'll do it myself," said the lad, trying to refuse and feeling faint pangs of dizziness. But drunken Seidakhmat wouldn't listen. He thought he was doing a good deed since the lad had been left alone at home and the day was that rare one with a full bowl, full spoon and full mouth . . .

Shakily, the lad followed Seidakhmat out of the house. In

the mountains it was a windy, partly cloudy day. The clouds drifted quickly across the sky and the weather twice changed sharply while the lad walked across the veranda: from an unbearably bright sunny day to unpleasant duskiness. The lad sensed this and it made his head ache. Driven on by a gust of wind, the smell of a wood fire struck him in the face. His eyes smarted. "They're probably doing the laundry today," he thought, for they usually made a fire in the yard on the day of a large wash, when the water was heated for all three houses in a huge black cauldron. One person couldn't lift this cauldron alone; Aunt Bekai and Guljamal managed it together.

The lad liked the big wash. For one thing, there was the fire in the open fireplace—you could play around with the flames, not like at home. Secondly, it was very entertaining to hang up the washed laundry. The lad also liked to steal up to the laundry hanging on a line and touch the wet cloth with his cheek.

This time, there was no laundry at all in the yard. But a great fire had been built under the big pot, and thick steam spewed up from the boiling vessel which was filled to its lip with big pieces of meat. The meat had already boiled down; its scent and the smell of the fire tickled the lad's senses and made him salivate. In a new red dress, new calf boots and a flowery light shawl thrown over her shoulders, Aunt Bekai was bending over the pot and draining off the foam with a ladle. And near her—standing on his knees—grandfather Momun poked at the hot logs in the fireplace.

"There he is, your grandfather," said Seidakhmat to the lad. "Let's go." And he'd hardly broken into his

> From the ginger-ginger mountains,
> I arrived on a ginger colt . . .

when Orozkul — head shaved, an axe in his hand and his shirt-sleeves rolled up — appeared from inside the shed.

"Where've you been?" he called menacingly to Seidakhmat. "Our guest over here is splitting firewood" — he nodded towards the driver, who was working away at some logs — "and you're singing songs."

"Aw, we'll take care of that in a jiffy," Seidakhmat mollified him and headed towards the driver. "Give it here, brother. I'll do it myself."

The lad moved closer to his grandfather, who was still on his knees near the fireplace. He approached him from behind.

"*Ata*," he said.

Grandfather didn't hear.

"*Ata*," the lad repeated, touching his grandfather on the shoulder. The old man glanced back and the lad didn't recognise him. Grandfather was also drunk. The lad couldn't remember when he'd seen his grandfather even slightly tight. If it ever happened, it could only be at some funeral feast of Issik-Kul elders, where vodka is handed out to everyone, even the women. But just like this, for no reason — it had never yet happened with grandfather.

The old man directed a kind of strange, detached, frantic look at the lad. His face was hot and red and when he recognised his grandson, it reddened even more. It flushed with a flaming colour, then instantly blanched. Grandfather hurriedly got to his feet.

"What is it, eh?" he said hollowly, pressing his grandson to him. "What is it, eh? What is it?" Except for these words, he could pronounce nothing, as if he'd lost the gift of speech. His agitation was transmitted to the lad.

"Are you sick, *Ata*?" he asked anxiously.

"Oh no, I'm just ... it's nothing," mumbled grandfather Momun. "You go on, have a little walk. I'll take care of the firewood here, I mean ..."

He almost pushed his grandson from him and, as if recoiling from the entire world, turned again to face the fireplace. He was on his knees; he did not look about him—didn't look at anything—but remained engrossed only in himself and the fire. The old man didn't see his grandson lounging about in bewilderment and walking across the yard towards Seidakhmat, who was busy cutting wood.

The lad didn't understand what had happened to his grandfather or what was taking place in the yard. It was only when he came nearer to the shed that he noticed a big mound of fresh red meat heaped up in a pile. It was on a hide stretched out on the ground, fur down. Pale little streams of blood were still oozing from the edges of the hide. Not far away, where the rubbish was usually thrown, the dog was shaking the entrails, rumbling with pleasure. Near the pile of meat, a stranger of some kind, a huge dark man, sat on his haunches like a lump. This was Koketai. He and Orozkul were carving the meat with knives in their hands. Leisurely, they tossed dismembered joints with the attached meat into various places on the stretched hide.

"What joy! And this wonderful smell," said the dark, hefty muzhik in a deep bass while sniffing at the meat.

"Take some more. Go on—take," Orozkul offered him generously. "Toss it onto your pile. God's given it to us from his herd in honour of your visit. It doesn't happen every day."

Orozkul puffed at this statement and got up occasionally to stroke his taut stomach, as if he'd had a huge meal of something; it was immediately evident that he'd already had a great deal to drink. Puffing huskily and feeling stifled, he tossed his head to draw breath. Fleshy like a cow's udders, his face was glossy with smugness and satiation.

The lad was struck dumb and overcome by a wave of cold when he saw the horned head of a maral beneath a wall of the shed. The severed head lay about in the dust, saturated with dark blood-stains. It looked like a snag tossed from a road. Four legs, severed at the knee joint, were scattered around the head.

The lad stared with horror at this frightful scene. He did not believe his eyes. The head of Horned Deer-Mother lay before him. He wanted to run away from this spectacle but his legs did not obey him. He stood and gazed at the dead, disfigured head of the white maral. The very same creature who was Horned Deer-Mother only yesterday, who regarded him from the other bank with a kind fixed gaze; the very same with whom he'd talked in his thoughts and whom he'd implored to bring a magic cradle with a little bell on her horns. All this had suddenly turned into a shapeless heap of meat, a flayed hide, severed legs and a head flung away over there.

It was absolutely essential for the lad to leave, yet he stood there as if petrified, unable to comprehend how and why all this had happened. The dark, hefty muzhik, the man who was carving up the meat, speared a kidney from the pile with the tip of his knife and held it out to the lad.

"Here, laddie, roast it on the coals, it'll be delicious," he said.

The lad didn't budge.

"Take it!" ordered Orozkul.

Feeling nothing, the lad put out his hand and stood there, tightly gripping Horned Deer-Mother's tender, still-warm kidney in his cold hand. Meanwhile, Orozkul lifted the head of the white maral by its horns.

"My word, it's heavy," he said, bouncing it up and down to gauge its weight. "The horns alone weigh a ton."

He propped up the head sideways on a chopping block, picked up the axe and set about hacking the horns from the skull.

"What horns!" he kept repeating while plunging the cutting edge of the axe into the base of the horns with a crunch. "This is for your grandfather." He winked to the lad. "When he croaks, we'll stick the horns on his grave. Then let anybody try to say we didn't respect him. What better respect? For these horns it wouldn't be a mistake to die straightaway, today!" Taking aim with the axe, he chuckled.

The horns wouldn't submit. Chopping them off turned out to be not so easy. The sodden Orozkul kept missing his mark, which enraged him. The head fell from the block and he began to chop at it while it lay on the ground. The head bounced away and Orozkul chased after it with the axe.

The lad shuddered, moving back on his heels involuntarily each time – but couldn't make himself leave. As in a nightmare, riveted in place by some sinister and incomprehensible power, he stood there and marvelled that Horned Deer-Mother's unblinking eye did not try to avoid the axe. It neither flinched nor cringed from fear. The head had been dragged through mud and dust for some time now but the eye remained clear and seemed still to look at the world with the mute, stupefied astonishment in which death found it. The lad was afraid that drunken Orozkul would land a blow in the eye.

Still the horns did not submit. Orozkul became more and more infuriated and wild; and not bothering to take aim now, he whacked at random at the head, using the butt of the axe as well as its blade.

"Wait, you'll smash the horns like that," said Seidakhmat, approaching. "Give it to me."

"Keep off. I'll do it myself," said Orozkul hoarsely, waving the axe. "Like hell I'll smash them up."

"All right, as you like," spat Seidakhmat, now heading towards his house. The same dark, hefty muzhik followed him, dragging his share of the meat in a big bag.

With drunken obstinacy, Orozkul continued to quarter Horned Deer-Mother's head behind the shed. One might have thought he was discharging a long awaited act of revenge.

"You bastard, you! You whore, you!" he shouted, foaming

at the mouth and kicking the head with his boot as if the dead object could hear him. "No no, you won't make a fool of me!" He attacked again and again with the axe. "If I don't finish you off, I won't be who I am. Take this. And this!" He smashed away with the axe. The skull cracked and splinters of bone flew in all directions.

The boy screamed briefly when the axe happened to land across the eye. A dark, thick liquid gushed out of the cleaved eye-socket. The eye died, disappeared, emptied...

"I can smash heads better than you are. And split off better horns," growled Orozkul in a paroxysm of wild malice and hatred of the innocent head.

At last he succeeded in staving in the skull at the forehead and top of the head. He threw away the axe, took a grip on the horns with both hands and, pressing the head to the ground with his foot, twisted at the horns with savage strength. When he tore them out they crackled, like ripped-out roots. These were the same horns on which, according to the lad's entreaties, Horned Deer-Mother was to have brought a magic cradle to Orozkul and Aunt Bekai.

The lad felt like fainting. He turned, dropped the kidney on the ground and slowly dragged himself away. He was very much afraid that he'd fall or vomit right there, in front of everybody. Pallid, with a cold, sticky perspiration on his forehead, he walked past the fireplace in which flames were shooting up fiercely and over which hot steam from the kettle was curling. And at which wretched grandfather Momun sat as before, his back turned to everyone, his face towards the fire. The lad decided not to trouble his grandfather. He wanted to get to his bed as quickly as he could, lie down and pull the covers over his head. To see nothing and hear nothing —to forget.

Aunt Bekai ran into him on the way. Dolled up preposterously—but with purplish-blue traces of Orozkul's beating on her face—she had been dashing around all day, lean and inappropriately gay, on errands for the 'big meat'.

She stopped the lad. "What's wrong with you?"

"My head hurts," he said.

"Oh my sweet little silly one," she said suddenly in a wave of tenderness. And began to shower him with kisses.

She too was drunk and reeked repellently of vodka.

"His head hurts," she mumbled affectedly. "My little darling, my own. You're probably hungry."

"No, I'm not hungry. I want to lie down."

"All right, let's go, I'll put you to bed. What are you going to do, lying all alone? Everybody's going to be at our place, you see. The guests, the whole family. And the meat's already done." She pulled him with her. When they passed the fireplace again, Orozkul appeared from behind the shed, stewed and red like an inflamed udder. Near grandfather Momun, he triumphantly dropped the maral horns that he'd hacked off. The old man rose from his place.

Not looking at him, Orozkul lifted a bucket of water, turned it up towards his face, and began to drink, spilling water down his front.

"Now you can croak," he tossed off, tearing himself from the water and again falling upon the bucket. The lad heard his grandfather babble.

"Thank you, my son. Thank you. Now I'm not afraid to die. Why should I be?—with this honour for me, I guess you'd call it, and this respect."

"I'm going home," said the lad, feeling weak up and down his body.

Aunt Bekai did not listen to him.

"You've nothing to do at home all alone." And she took him into her house almost by force, settling him on a bed in the corner.

In Orozkul's house, everything was already ready for the

feast. Boiled, fried and roasted. Old grandma and Guljamal saw to all this with great animation. Aunt Bekai scurried on errands between the house and the fireplace in the yard. While waiting for the 'big meat', Orozkul and the dark, hefty Koketai took their pleasure in some tea, half lying on flowery blankets with pillows under their elbows. They had quickly put on high-horse airs and deported themselves like princes. Seidakhmat poured the tea for them into little drinking-bowls.

The lad lay quietly in the corner, tense and constrained. He was feverish again. He wanted to get up and leave, but was afraid that if he stood up from the bed, he'd vomit immediately. Therefore he convulsively held tight to the lump stuck in his throat, afraid to make an unnecessary move.

Soon the women called Seidakhmat into the yard, and he appeared back at the door with a mountain of steaming meat in a huge enamel bowl. He carried his burden with difficulty and set it before Orozkul and Koketai. Following him, the women carried in various other things to eat.

Everyone began to settle himself into a place, while knives and plates were made ready. While this was taking place, Seidakhmat poured vodka into the water-glasses.

"I'll be captain of the vodka," he roared with laughter and nodded at the bottles in a corner.

Grandfather Momun came in last. The old man had a queer, too-pitiful look today, even compared to his ordinary appearance. He wanted to squeeze in somewhere on the side, but dark, hefty Koketai magnanimously asked him to sit at his side.

"Come through over here, *Aksakal*."

"Thanks, we'll stay here," grandfather Momun tried to refuse. "We're at home, after all."

"But you're the oldest all the same," insisted Koketai, seating him between himself and Seidakhmat. "Let's drink to your success, *Aksakal*. You have the first toast."

Grandfather Momun cleared his throat uncertainly.

"To peace in this house," he managed to force out. "Where there's peace, there's happiness, my children."

"That's right, absolutely right," everyone joined in, tossing down his glass.

"And what about you?" Koketai reproached the embarrassed grandfather Momun. "No, that won't do. You wish happiness for your son-in-law and daughter—then don't drink yourself."

"Well if it's really for happiness, what can I say?" the old man hastened to pronounce. To everyone's surprise, he gulped down almost an entire water-glass of vodka to the bottom. Stunned, he began to shake his old head.

"Bravo!"

"Our old man tops them all!"

"Your old man's smashing!"

Everyone laughed, everyone was pleased, everyone praised grandfather.

It became hot and stuffy in the house. The lad lay in pain, feeling sick the entire time. He lay with his eyes open and heard the people champing, gnawing and puffing while stuffing themselves on Horned Deer-Mother's meat—heard them offering each other tasty pieces, clinking soiled glasses and tossing the picked bones into a bowl.

"This isn't meat, it's a young little colt," boasted Koketai, smacking his lips.

"What are we, asses or something?" said Orozkul. "To live in the mountains and not eat meat like this!"

"That's right, that's why we live here," echoed Seidakhmat.

Everyone lauded Horned Deer-Mother's meat. Old grandma, Aunt Bekai, Guljamal and even grandfather Momun. They also poked at the boy and served him some meat and other things on a plate. But he refused, and when they saw that he wasn't well, the drunken celebrants left him in peace.

The lad lay on the bed, clenching his teeth. It seemed to him that this would help him cope with his nausea. But he was tormented even more by the recognition of his own helplessness—that he was powerless to do anything with these people who had killed Horned Deer-Mother. And in his righteous child's wrath—and his desperation—he dreamed up various kinds of vengeance: how he punished them and made them understand what a heinous crime they had committed. But he could think of nothing better than to call for Kulubek's help in his imagination. Yes, the very same fellow in the army field-jacket who'd come for the hay with the young drivers on that stormy night. He was the only person of all the lad knew who could overpower Orozkul and tell him the whole truth straight to his face.

At the lad's summons, Kulubek rushed there in his lorry and jumped out of the cab with a tommy-gun at the ready. "Where are they?" "They're over there." Together, they ran to Orozkul's house and flung open the door. "Don't make a move. Hands up!" ordered Kulubek threateningly from the doorstep, aiming the tommy-gun. They all lost their wits; everyone froze with fear where he sat. Pieces of food stuck in their gullets. With joints in their greasy hands, with greasy cheeks and fatty mouths, gorged and drunk, they couldn't even budge.

"All right, get up, you swine!" Kulubek thrust the tommy-gun to Orozkul's temple, and the latter, trembling all over and stuttering, fell at Kulubek's feet. "Have mercy, d-don't kill m-m-me." But Kulubek was implacable. "Get outside, you swine. This is your end." With a sharp kick, he prodded Orozkul in his fatty bum and forced him up and out of the house. Everyone else went out into the yard, fearful and mute.

"Up against the wall," Kulubek ordered Orozkul. "For killing Horned Deer-Mother, for chopping off her horns on which she brought the cradle—you'll die." Orozkul fell into the dust and began to crawl, howl and groan. "Don't kill me, I don't even have children. I'm alone in the whole world, I don't have a son or a daughter..."

So much for his arrogance and his conceit. He was a miserable, measly coward. You don't even want to kill his kind.

"Okay, we won't kill him," the lad said to Kulubek. "But get this man out of here and see he never returns. He's not wanted here. Let him clear out."

Orozkul got up, pulled up his trousers and, too frightened to look around, trotted away—fat, flabby and in sagging breeches. But Kulubek stopped him. "Wait. We'll tell you one last thing. You'll never have children. You're a wicked, worthless man. Nobody likes you here. The forest doesn't like you, not a single tree does—not a single blade of grass. You're a fascist. Clear out—and make it forever. And you'd better be fast." Orozkul ran off without looking back. "*Schnell, schnell,*" Kulubek laughed after him, firing the tommy-gun into the air to scare him.

The lad rejoiced. And after Orozkul disappeared from sight, Kulubek told the others, who were standing guiltily at the door. "How did you put up with such a man? Aren't you ashamed of yourselves?"

The lad felt a sense of relief. A just trial had been carried out. And he so believed his dream that he forgot where he was and on what occasion people were drinking themselves drunk in Orozkul's house.

A spasm of laughter brought him back from this blissful state. The lad opened his eyes and listened. Grandfather Momun wasn't in the room—he'd probably gone out somewhere. The women were clearing away the dishes and preparing to serve tea. Seidakhmat was describing something loudly and the others were laughing at his words.

"And what then?"

"Go on, give us more."

"No listen, you tell us—repeat it again," asked Orozkul, almost dying of laughter. "What did you tell him about that thing? How'd you scare him? Oh, I can't take any more."

"Well it was like this . . ." Seidakhmat willingly undertook to repeat what he had already described. "As soon as we began to ride up to the marals—they were at the forest's edge, all three. As soon as we tied up the horses to some trees, the old man of mine suddenly grabs me by the arm. 'We can't shoot the marals,' he says. 'We're Buguans, the children of Horned Deer-Mother.' And he looks at me like a baby. Begging with his eyes. And me, I can't even stand on my feet, I'm breaking up with laughter. But I keep myself from laughing. Just the opposite, I play it real serious, 'What are you up to?' I say. 'You looking to spend some time in the clink?' 'No,' he says. 'But you know that *bai* fairy-tales were dreamt up in the dark *bai* days to, er, scare the poorly people.' Then his mouth opens. 'You don't say,' he says. 'Just you remember that,' I say, 'and drop all your crazy nursery stories. Or else I'll forget you're an old man and report about you to the right places.' "

"Haw, haw, haw," the others burst into laughter in unison. Orozkul most of all, for he savoured his laughter.

"So, then we steal up to them. Any other animal would have beat it out of there fast without a trace—but these half-witted marals don't run, you'd think they weren't afraid of us. So all the better, I think," boasted the drunken Seidakhmat. "I went ahead with the rifle. The old man followed behind. But now I began to have some doubts. I never shot a sparrow in my life—and now we had this thing to take care of. I'd probably miss, and then they'd dart through the forest and we'd have to track them down. It's no joke trying to keep up with them. And who'd want to miss a chance at game like that? But the old man's a hunter—he's dealt with bear in his time. So I say to him, here's the rifle, old man—you shoot. But he won't do it for anything; shoot yourself, he says. So I tell him, I'm all pickled, I say. And I make myself stagger as if I can hardly stand on my feet. He'd seen himself when we dragged the log out of the river — we all downed a bottle together. So that's the game I played."

"Haw, haw, haw."

"I'll miss, I tell him. The marals will get away and won't come back a second time. And you and I better not come back empty-handed. You know that yourself. Don't you forget it. Why were we sent out here? He says nothing. And won't take the rifle. Okay, I say, if that's the way you want it. I dropped the rifle and made like I was leaving. He follows me. It's all the same to me, I say: if Orozkul throws me out, I'll get a job on the state farm. But what about you in your old age? He still says nothing. And I start off nice and easy — for the effect, that is.

> From the ginger-ginger mountains,
> I arrived on a ginger colt,
> Hey ginger dealer, open the door..."

"Haw, haw, haw."

"He swallows it, thinks I'm really drunk. He goes to get the rifle. I turn back too. While we were arguing, the marals of ours had pushed on a bit farther. 'Now you look sharp,' I say, 'they'll get away and you won't catch up. Shoot while they're not scared.' The old man picked up the rifle. He began to creep up closer. And he keeps whispering, like an idiot: 'Forgive me, Horned Deer-Mother, forgive me...' And I'm at him with my line: watch out, I say, you'll slip up — and if you do, you can take off with the marals and follow your nose; you'd better not come back."

"Haw, haw, haw."

In the chortling and drunken fumes, the lad felt more and

more hot and suffocated. His head split from ever-swelling pain which would not stay inside its limits. It seemed to him that someone was kicking his head with his feet, that someone was chopping at his head with an axe. It seemed to him that someone was taking aim at his eyes with an axe and he jerked his head away in an attempt to dodge the blow. Fainting from the heat, he suddenly found himself in the ice-cold river. He had turned into a fish. The tail, body and fins—he was entirely a fish; only his head remained his own—and still ached. He swam in dark, muffled underwater coolness and thought about how he'd remain a fish forever now and never return to the mountains. "I won't come back," he said to himself, "it's better that I be a fish."

Behind the windows of Orozkul's house, drunken voices roared and shouted. The boorish haw-hawing deafened the boy and brought him unbearable pain and torment. It seemed to him that it was this appalling laughter that made him ill. Recovering his breath, he walked across the yard. It was deserted. Near the dying fire, the lad came upon grandfather Momun, deathly drunk. The old man was lying in the dust near Horned Deer-Mother's severed horns. The dog was chewing at the stump of the maral's head.

The lad roved farther. He went down to the river. And stepped directly into the water. Hurrying, slipping and falling, he ran across the shallows, shivering from the icy spray—and when he reached the rapids, the current knocked him off his feet. Floundering in the turbulent torrent, he swam, choking and freezing.

The lad swam down the river, at times face up, other times face down; sometimes being held back near piles of stones, other times rushing towards the waterfalls . . .

No one yet knew that the lad was swimming as a fish down the river. The drunken song sounded in the yard.

> From the hunch-backed, hunch-backed mountains,
> I arrived on a hunch-backed camel,
> Hey, hunch-backed dealer, open the door
> We'll drink some bitter wine ...

This song you no longer heard. You were swimming, my lad, into your tale. Did you know that you would never turn into a fish, not reach the Issik-Kul, not see the white steamship and say to it, "Hello, white steamship, it's me!"

You swam.

I can only say one thing now: you rejected what your child's heart could not reconcile itself to. And that's my consolation. You lived like a bolt of lightning which once—and only once—flashed and expired. But lightning strikes from the sky. And the sky is eternal. This too is my consolation. And that a child's conscience in a person is like an embryo in a particle of grain: the grain won't grow without the embryo. That whatever awaits us on earth, truth will endure forever, as long as people are born and die.

Taking leave of you, my lad, I repeat your own words. "Hello, white steamship, it's me."

Afterword

by
Tatyana and George Feifer

CHINGIZ AITMATOV is one of the most pivotal figures in contemporary Soviet literature. Still called a 'younger writer', he is acclaimed by Politburo members in the same breath with the most honoured names of Soviet letters. A member of a remote and relatively unlettered national minority, his best-known works have been written in Russian and widely praised for language and style. Warmly admired by young Russian intellectuals with a deep suspicion of 'establishment' literature, he himself is a solid pillar of the establishment, one of a handful of writers permitted to travel in the West. Published in 'Novy Mir' when that most respected of Russia's literary magazines sustained the hopes of Russian liberals, he was enthusiastically reviewed by 'Oktyabr', the ultra-orthodox opponent of liberal voices. "He seems to be a sort of consensus author, a rare bird on the stressful Soviet literary scene," an English critic has written in an attempt to fix his position. "In short, a man who even the most diplomatic of Soviet cultural diplomats could be really happy to recommend to Westerners."

That Aitmatov defies easy categorisation speaks not only of the limitations of some of the standard approaches to classifying Soviet writers but also of his unusual blend of background, achievements and recognition—and, above all, of his talent and originality. At a time when published Soviet fiction, burdened with severe ideological demands, rarely interests Russian intellectuals themselves, Aitmatov's artistic voice rings out in contrast to the general mumble, and has won him genuine popularity among the most discriminating reading public, simultaneously with his illustrious official honours.

To some extent, Aitmatov's background explains his originality and his success. He was born forty-five years ago in a small Kirghizian settlement in the foothills of the Tien Sham mountains, just below a vast desert-like area called Golodnaya Steppe ('Hungry Steppe'). Three hundred miles west, amidst some of the Soviet Union's highest mountains, nestles the great Issik-Kul. The area as a whole lies almost two thousand miles south-east of Moscow at the far edge of Soviet Central Asia, where the sparsely settled Kirghiz Soviet Socialist Republic forms the border with China. Of the million-odd Kirghizians, most are descendants of nomadic tribes once headed by feudal chieftains, and many now raise sheep and horses on collective farms. The geographic and climatic conditions—rugged mountains and parched steppes, both subject to extremes of temperature—are those of 'The White Steamship'.

John French, Aitmatov's translator and friend, has learned something of the writer's family background and early years.

> The root of his family name—Aitmat—means tailor. His grandfather, who was a famous craftsman in metal and leather, especially in the making of saddles, had brought the first sewing machine to [the family's settlement of] Sheker. But in spite of this skill and his fame as a player of the national instrument, the 'komuz', he remained poor. However, his son had the opportunity of learning Russian and later studied in Moscow. Thus Chingiz Aitmatov's parents, and especially his mother, taught him Russian and introduced him at an early age to Russian literature. At the same time, the young Chingiz's grandmother on his father's side taught him Kirghiz and the wealth of legend, songs and lore of his

Kirghiz people. On her death, his aunt continued this part of his education. Then he went to schools, both Russian and Kirghiz. Because of the war, in 1942 he had to leave school early in order to help his mother bring up her four children. He worked in various posts in Sheker on the village's collective farm. Then he went to the veterinary school at Dzhambul, across the border in Kazakhstan, from which he graduated with honours. Later he passed out from the Kirghiz Agricultural Institute as a livestock specialist or 'zootekhnik' in 1953. While at the Institute he began his literary career by translating one of the Soviet author Kataev's books into Kirghiz. In 1952 he published his first story — about a Japanese newsboy — 'Newsboy Dzhyuido'.

Four years later, Aitmatov left farming to enter the Higher Course of Literature of the Writers' Union in Moscow. He was graduated from the two-year programme in 1958, having published three novellae after 'Newsboy Dzhyuido'. Since then, he has written stories, novellae and sketches in both Russian and Kirghiz, and translated from both languages into the other. He has also worked as a 'Pravda' correspondent and the editor of a Kirghiz literary magazine. His prose has been adapted for stage and screen — a film entitled 'The First Teacher' after the story of the same name won high praise in the West as well as in Russia — and he himself has written screenplays. Clearly Kirghizia's first writer, he is, as Soviet leaders proudly boast, a cultural 'achievement' of national and even international importance.

His earliest stories, even those which betrayed signs of a young writer learning his craft, stood out invitingly from the bulk of Soviet fiction. Russian readers were attracted by a fresh voice, striking images and a gripping 'sincerity'. Although occasionally rough and lacking his later creativity — the use of folk legends and ancient word roots to sustain a poetic, 'primitive' atmosphere — his style was highly expressive and indicated thorough schooling in Gorky, Fadeev and other 'teachers' of socialist realism. His narratives too were compelling, not only because they brought an unfamiliar background vividly to life but also through Aitmatov's talent for creating believable characters involved in sharp social and emotional conflict, as opposed to the contrived situations of much of Soviet fiction. 'Face to Face' (1957) is the story of a Second World War deserter who returns to his wife in a Kirghiz village and is hidden by her, despite misgivings, because of her love and devotion. In the end, the young woman turns her husband in because he has shown himself a thoroughly selfish and cruel man, heedless of the villagers' extreme privation. The conflict between her love and her social responsibilities is depicted with great sharpness, and her rebellion against her husband's domination is significant in view of the powerful Central Asian tradition of wives' submissiveness.

'Dzamilia' (1958), the tale of a young married woman in love with another man, shows the influence of Gorky in his stories of strong-willed women winning the courage to liberate themselves in affairs of the heart. According to custom, Dzamilia is living with her husband's family, again in a Kirghiz village, while the husband himself is fighting at the front; eventually, she breaks with tradition and goes off with the gentle young man she loves. In 'Farewell, Gul'sary!' (1966), the setting is again Kirghizia, but this time the social and political significance is much greater. Watching his beloved horse Gul'sary die, an old man spends a bleak night alone on a mountain road, remembering the adversities of their lives. He had been a fervent young revolutionary who, not without ruthlessness for the sake of the socialist future, played an important role in organising his collective farm and stifling resistance to it. But the local Party leadership (under Stalin's reign) is taken over by hateful men who, together with the severe climatic conditions and pitiful shortage of food and supplies, subject the struggling farm to extraordinary hardships. Far from enjoying the fruits of his efforts and sacrifices, the old collective farmer is broken in every way and expelled from the Party, an act of injustice crowning a shameful series of them by the local Party tyrants.

'Farewell, Gul'sary!' approached the limit of the permissible in treatment of national heritage and history, and was particularly revealing about the desolating fate of many revolutionaries of the 1920s and 1930s whose dreams of the socialist future—surely similar to Aitmatov's own—and self-sacrificial labours brought them a special grief under Stalinism. As an English observer remarked, Aitmatov 'no doubt did as much justice to history as may be seen to be done in the present state of Soviet society'. The novel also encouraged the Hungarian Georg Lukacs, perhaps the most influential Marxist literary critic, to hope for a renaissance of Russian literature and return to 'human and artistic perspectives' and the greatness of socialist realism in its first flowering after the Revolution. Lukacs felt that very occasionally, as in this instance, social criticism expressed in published Soviet fiction went beyond even Solzhenitsyn's.[1]

In other respects, however, Aitmatov and Solzhenitsyn are poles apart, and to think of them as confederates is to join the school of criticism which assumes that talent and originality, not to speak of social criticism, 'ipso facto' put a writer in the 'dissident' category. In fact, Aitmatov is far closer to the literary establishment's general staff, with its bureaucratic procedures and domination of every published word, than to the literary underground which circulates unauthorised, dog-eared manuscripts hand-to-hand. When Solzhenitsyn was expelled from the Writers' Union in 1969, Aitmatov was, as he still is, a member of the Union's governing board. When Solzhenitsyn addressed his celebrated protest and appeal for literature's liberation to the Fourth Congress of Soviet Writers two years earlier, Aitmatov was a member of the Congress's

---

[1] 'Farewell, Gul'sary!', Lukacs wrote, shows "the way in which the brutal bureaucratic manipulation of the Stalin system turned against those who ... had worked enthusiastically to bring about the socialist revolution, undaunted by the sacrifices demanded of them. We see how, until their own tragic downfall, they were able to preserve their human commitment to the revolution in the midst of the destruction of their own existence." 'Solzhenitsyn', Georg Lukacs (London, Merlin Press, 1970).

presidium which put liberals in despair by blankly ignoring both Solzhenitsyn and his momentous issues. Many Russian intellectuals are convinced that Aitmatov is doing much to improve the integrity of Soviet letters, but his way is hardly Solzhenitsyn's.[1]

Awards, honours and position have been consistently bestowed upon Aitmatov. Laureate of both Lenin and State Prizes for Literature, he serves on the editorial boards of 'Novy Mir', and 'Literaturnaya Gazetta', the most prominent literary newspaper.[2] *In a country which lavishes as many titles and privileges on approved artists as harassment and punishment upon the disfavoured, he has become a personage of the political as well as literary establishment: the People's Writer of the Kirghiz Republic is also a deputy to the Supreme Soviet.*

For years, he has been held up as an example to Soviet writers. When Yevgeny Yevtushenko, Vasily Aksyonov and Andrei Voznesensky were under attack in the mid-1960s for forgetting that "there can be no question of any kind of co-existence between the ideological positions of the socialist and capitalist worlds", Aitmatov was cited to them as a young writer whose irreproachable ideological rectitude did not stop him from making 'fresh and brilliant observations'. When 'Novy Mir' was censured for insufficient patriotism and 'Sovietism' by orthodox magazines with a high-pitched zeal for

---

[1] *Nor would Aitmatov make any such claim. On a trip to London in 1970, he told an interviewer he felt it 'quite possible' that Solzhenitsyn might be published again in 'Novy Mir'—'if Solzhenitsyn wrote some outstanding new book that would contribute something positive to the development of our society'. Even discounting the well-known pressures on a Soviet writer permitted to travel to the West, Aitmatov's answer indicates little sympathy for Solzhenitsyn's stance or the great novels that won him the Nobel Prize. If a parallel must be found for Aitmatov's position in Soviet letters, he seems much closer to Yevgeny Yevtushenko in the sense that he works, 'within' 'the system' to publish his sometimes startling works and perhaps even plays the game of producing an occasional article or speech which, because their patriotic and ideological emphasis can be calculated to please conservative cultural overseers, might help him win more artistic and thematic leeway for important projects. Still, Aitmatov has been considerably less adventurous and startling, therefore less controversial, than Yevtushenko too.*

[2] *He is also chairman of the board of Kirghizia's Union of Cinematographers.*

protecting Marxist-Leninism from the danger of 'alien ideological influences', Aitmatov was singled out as a 'Novy Mir' writer whom 'we all hold dear'. When writers belonging to non-Russian national minorities were rebuked for nationalistic tendencies—for failing to understand national sentiment's proper place in a socialist society— Aitmatov's work was cited as an example of the 'correct approach': literature showing 'Leninist friendship of the peoples in action . . . [and] . . . the genuine triumph of the nationalities policy in our Soviet land'.[1] In his day, Nikita Khrushchev praised Aitmatov extravagantly, but no more so than Leonid Brezhnev who, in an appeal for greater attention to ideology in the classroom, included Aitmatov with Gorky, Mayakovsky, Sholokhov and Alexei Tolstoy and other writers who were a worthy inspiration. Everywhere, the Soviet press echoed 'Izvestiya's' praise of 'the young Kirghizian writer's profound, poetic narratives' and his 'craving to understand and create understanding for the homeland in the most complex periods of its historical existence'. From the days when he served as Young Communist organiser for forums of young writers, hardly a literary conference or symposium passed without an appearance by or mention of him; everywhere his talent was celebrated as a 'triumph of Leninist aesthetic principles'.

Several qualities have earned Aitmatov this unstinting official favour. Most important, he did in fact manage to make 'fresh observations' without in any way stepping outside the boundaries of socialist realism. And he consistently and outspokenly supported the general aims of Soviet cultural philosophy as well as its occasional sharp fluctuations. When Nikita Khrushchev's celebrated outburst at an exhibition of faintly abstractionist paintings launched a violent crusade for renewed vigilance in the arts, Aitmatov joined the

[1] *In other words, Aitmatov had portrayed the Kirghiz people as thankful for its association with Moscow and full of good feeling towards the Russian people because its legitimate national aspirations were satisfied within the structure of the Soviet Union. However, this view is apparently far from universal in the Republic, where even official newspapers have criticised Aitmatov for being too 'Russian' and forgetting his native land.*

writers who acclaimed the crusade's righteousness, writing in 'Pravda' of 'N. S. Khrushchev's brilliant and concise speech which constituted a stirring event in the history of Soviet culture' and publicly chiding Yevtushenko, Aksyonov and Voznesensky, 'whose creative work has been subjected to justified Party criticism'.[1]

As for himself, he proudly proclaimed his commitment to Party goals, making speech after ardent speech that would earn him the epithet 'Young Communist type' (roughly 'Boy-Scout type') among Russian contemporaries who had lost their fervour. At writers' conferences, he appealed both for improvement of artistic standards and for discharge of ideological responsibilities. He did not try to deny the difficulties in living up to high Party principles and applying them to literature, especially of interesting the public with fiction based on 'truth and conviction' rather than scepticism and sensationalism. Nor was he blind to the scepticism that inevitably greeted his own somewhat old-fashioned dedication. "I know now," he interjected during a speech to assembled writers, "that someone will be thinking to himself: 'Here's one more "ideological comrade" from Central Asia.' Well, let him think what he likes. I've long been acquainted with this ironical 'ideological comrade' tag, ever since my days at the Literature Institute."

Again discounting any pressures on Soviet writers speaking from tribunes, all the circumstances of Aitmatov's address, together with its patent earnestness, encourage the outsider to feel that his self-categorisation was accurate. Knowledge of his background and rise to prominence gives one even less reason to question his sincerity.

Life has acquainted me with every kind of comrade. And I am on

[1] However, Aitmatov's criticism was far gentler than ultra-conservatives', and although he need not have joined the condemnation at all if he were determined not to, in one sense he tried to defend his 'wayward' colleagues. "I only want to say," he declared at a meeting summoned to denounce ideological weakness, "that I have a certain amount of respect for the literary capabilities of Yevtushenko, Aksyonov and others"—and it was precisely because of this respect that he wished they would face their responsibilities as writers.

the side of those ideological comrades who since 1953 have been able to outlive the bitterness of the past under the cult of the individual [the Stalin era] and have been able to link their destiny with the destiny of the people and the Party. I am on the side of those ideological comrades who, in these years, have lifted up agriculture, lifted up collective farmers and collective farms, and for this alone I am ready to serve the Party with truth and faith, because I know what it was like on the collective farms and what was happening. I am on the side of those who have built housing for all, including even the mocking sceptics, on the side of those who herd the flocks through snowstorms, who conquer the virgin lands, who build power plants. But I also know some who have grumbled all this time, who are discontent, who talk loudly in cabarets and laugh at our shortcomings and difficulties. For them, possibly, I really am a frightfully 'ideological' comrade, and if this is so, I am proud of it . . .

This commitment may help outsiders understand why the authorities warmly approved of Aitmatov despite the seeming political daring of some of his stories. Several years ago, 'Pravda' severely censured several stories of village life in which socialist ideals were distorted or ignored. To see their weaknesses, the Party newspaper explained, it was only necessary to compare them with 'Farewell, Gul'sary!' ('permeated with artistic truth') whose hero retains his burning faith in collectivised agriculture despite his far more severe hardships. Aitmatov, in other words, depicted sharp conflicts and difficulties—but resolved them correctly. The hardships of his 'The First Teacher' were also painful. Almost singlehandedly, a passionate young Bolshevik overcomes fearful obstacles to establish the first Soviet school in a Central Asian village, soon after the revolution. No attempt is made to hide the hostility of many of the tribesmen to Soviet rule or the young teacher's sometimes destructive excess of zeal. But he perseveres, learns, and wins in the end—a heroic but believable protagonist of whom Aitmatov has said, "Yes, in 'The First Teacher', I wanted to affirm our concept of the positive hero in literature, and I consciously idealised the image of the Communist's selfless devotion . . ."

This is what one knew about Aitmatov before the appearance of 'The White Steamship'. The publication—in the January 1970 issue of 'Novy Mir'—of the tale of grandfather Momun and his grandson put him in a new perspective. From a literary standpoint, in terms of both language and narrative, it is his most accomplished work. In perception too, it may be said to represent a distinct maturation, although Soviet readers and critics were hardly unanimous about this.

The novel's venture onto new ground—Aitmatov's failure to resolve the conflicts in his accustomed way—was quickly discerned by readers. One wrote to an editor in disappointment over the 'too great distance' between this work and Aitmatov's earlier ones. Another took issue more specifically with the ending. The narrator's comment on the final page seemed to indicate that this ending was fated—but could that really be? "Of course not. Not only life tells us [that another ending is possible] but Aitmatov himself—all his earlier books." Why had Aitmatov made the lad plunge into the river, thus awarding a 'victory' to pessimism over the beauty, truth, dreams and joy of his own novel?

Disturbed too by the ending, other readers questioned the novel's 'facts' and logic. "In the tale's narrative," wrote an engineer, "I tried to discern . . . natural logic, human and historical meaning. But alas, 'The White Steamship' did not gladden so much as grieve me." One reader drew attention to the lad's inherent gregariousness, and disputed that he could have had no friends to comfort him. "Where is it, that cordon—in what remote, ancient kingdom? How did it happen that [the lad] had neither school friends nor school activities?" This man went on to thank Aitmatov for his earlier stories which, 'whether pervaded with a lyrical mist of sadness or overflowing with the most profound dramatic qualities', were poetry in the 'highest and best sense of that word' and 'left me with a sense of joy—with the feeling that is called life-assertive'. This had held true even in the darkest and cruellest moments endured by Aitmatov's previous protagonists. "But suddenly, 'The White Steamship' appears, and so stuns me with its inconsolable ending that everything has become pitch-black."

It is not unusual for Russian readers, even prominent critics, to criticise a work of fiction for inaccurate 'facts'. The existence of an official-approved literary school (socialist realism) and of an obligatory social role assigned to all literature—reducing the doctrine to its simplest terms, literature is meant to encourage the Soviet people to follow the Party's leadership in building a Communist society—has led to fiction being judged by considerations which receive far less attention in the West.[1] Russian authors are virtually never accused of erring on the side of optimism, for there is strong pressure to emphasise the 'positive' and 'progressive' aspects of Soviet life which will inspire new efforts towards official goals. Treatment of 'negative' aspects is correspondingly less encouraged; and anything that might generate pessimism is deeply suspect. Only ultra-conservative critics accuse authors of 'helping our enemies', but many feel that a grim picture of this village or that, one incident or another serves to discourage the Soviet people—and in any case, is 'wrong' because untypical. Does Aitmatov mean to say that Soviet forest preserves in general are like Orozkul's? Why did he choose an aberration to describe instead of the norm? Does this not give a false picture of Soviet reality—and impede progress towards common aims? As a major magazine wrote much later in 'The White Steamship' 'affair', it is necessary and correct to 'examine any artistic creation not independently but on a wide historical background'. In other words,

---

[1] Some of Aitmatov's supporters, too, responded on the plane of the novel's 'accuracy'. In defence of the portrait of Orozkul, a journalist quoted from children's letters she kept in a special folder: descriptions of loutishness, drunkenness and beatings by fathers which had driven the children to despair. The raising of these matters indicates literature's continuing importance, even in its substantial restrictions, as Russia's principal vehicle for social debate.

a novel out of harmony with Marxist-Leninist ideals and the accepted view of Soviet history and society is not good literature, however talented in itself.

There was nothing unfamiliar in these attitudes as expressed towards 'The White Steamship'; what was new was the extent of disapproval the novel provoked. In Russia (as distinct from Kirghizia, where Aitmatov had apparently ruffled national feelings occasionally) this was Aitmatov's first work so greeted. But with understandable reason: it was his first work to lack a happy ending. Even in the deeply tragic 'Farewell, Gul'sary!', a 'good' Party secretary turned up at literally the last moment to breathe hope to the pitiably mistreated collective farmer and, through the secretary's assurances of the great changes since Stalin's death, to Aitmatov's readers. The contrast with 'The White Steamship' is striking: not only does no one turn up to save the lad, but he, unlike the collective farmer, has done nothing whatever in his young life to bring about his own hardships. He is that unfamiliar figure in contemporary Soviet fiction, a wholly innocent victim of social injustice which is 'not' righted in the end, but causes unmitigated grief; a hero who dies not in an inspiring struggle, but in despair. In this sense, the novel goes hard against the grain of the literary convention that tragic situations from which there is no successful, if not triumphant, outcome are not suitable subjects. And against the 'official' life-is-wonderful optimism that nurtures that convention. "She knows that however great her sadness," wrote a reader about an earlier Aitmatov protagonist, "life goes on and life is marvellous."

For all the naivety of some of the readers' letters, most raised the important questions, and for the most part, the critics—who also reacted in unusual volume and disaccord—offered elaborations of the same arguments, principally about the 'irremediable tragedy'. They too praised Aitmatov's talent, but questioned his judgment. "For all of the great emotional glow and poetic mood that distinguishes the Kirghizian author's latest work," wrote one, "it is not without its shortcomings." Like readers, critics lamented Aitmatov's deviation *from his earlier works, with their ability to 'illuminate the social significance of events' and inspire the reader with 'hopes and dreams'. "Reading 'The White Steamship'," another explained, "I involuntarily remember Chingiz Aitmatov's first [sic!] novella, 'Face to Face'. In something significant, it resembled 'The White Steamship'. In it too, there was a man similar to Orozkul: Ismail, the traitor to the Motherland. But at the same time, there is something that gives the narration a wholly different ring."*

One critic was particularly dismayed by Aitmatov's misinterpretation of the legend of Horned Deer-Mother. "But this lyric glorifying brotherly unity in peaceful toil and kinship with nature takes on an unjustifiable 'inconsolableness' in Chingiz Aitmatov's pen: it is as if only the gloomy prophecies of Lame Pock-marked Old Woman came true in the history of mankind. For was it not they which predetermined the lad's fate?"

Aitmatov's critics appeared deeply disturbed by what they considered fundamental errors in his perception. This was revealed perhaps even more clearly by the circumlocutory language to which some of them resorted. Thus Aitmatov was reprimanded for implying that 'beauty' (represented by the San-Tash cordon and poetry of his own descriptions) is incompatible with 'reality', the code word for Soviet life. He was charged with deviating from 'historical and social roots' — in other words, of creating a false picture of Soviet conditions, which cancelled out all the novel's spiritual qualities and made the experiment of using the legend 'lose all reason'. A careful examination of the region's real life — of the horse and sheep breeders, the lorry drivers and even the cordon, with the state farm a mere five kilometres away — shows that Aitmatov 'manifestly deviated from reality'.

The language of other critics was direct, however, and in their opposition to Aitmatov's use of the legend of Horned Deer-Mother, they seemed to be saying that tragic fairy-tales have little relevance to, or purpose for, the Soviet Union. The novel also stimulated a considerable discussion of the role of myths and mythology in

Soviet literature, in which some of the same general considerations — what application to socialist realism should be made of ancient treasures not, on the face of it, compatible with Marxism-Leninism — were grappled with. In his eagerness to assert the 'life-asserting' function of myths, one critic seemed to forget the fate of the marals in the legend of Horned Deer-Mother.

Is the artist correct who, having illuminated his work about our contemporary life with a thousand-year legend about the beautiful and the good, decides to elevate evil over light and beauty? For a work of art acquires an optimistic trend ... making all other interpretation impossible, only when its foundation lies in a battle against evil, and in the highest degree a 'social' battle on a 'grand scale', as it were. It is precisely this approach to the function of art that we see in the legend itself of Horned Deer-Mother, taken as the foundation of 'The White Steamship'. Was it wise to interpret it differently and to build a dam before its shining denouement, intended for us and our future? Because in the pen of such a bright talent as Chingiz Aitmatov, thanks to the strength of the reaction to his work, Orozkul's victory over Momun becomes a symbol of helplessness and darkness.

Predictably, the reaction to the novel by many Moscow intellectuals was very different. More admiring of Aitmatov than ever before, they were also somewhat surprised at the story's approval by censors during a restrictive period when demands for orthodoxy in literature are again insistent and strident. Apart from their appreciation of its literary qualities, liberal intellectuals saw in 'The White Steamship' a refreshing 'purity' — a freedom from cant and ideological imperatives — and rare stimulation for serious thoughts about contemporary Soviet society (of which some themes will be discussed below).

Nor, by any means, were all published letters and articles critical. "The book convinces me," wrote a doctor, "that all who read this wonderful tale will fight against every manifestation of evil and brute force, whatever form they take." "Yes," wrote another reader, "cruelty and spiritual emptiness, drunkenness and wickedness—these are terrible things. And [the novel] insists we do not forget this." A saddened woman wrote that 'all the same', she could not criticise the tragic ending, since 'books condemning evil with such force—evil which still exists and which we often ignore—are also much needed'. In defending the novel, some critics seemed to blunt its significance to make it more palatable. Thus, it was emphasised that the tragic situation was wholly local, pertaining to Orozkul's cordon only. ("*That which took place in the cordon with Momun took place with him alone.*") And that in this cordon, the losses of the war and hardships of the post-war period (which robbed the area of men) were largely responsible for the weakness of 'good' forces to oppose Orozkul's evil. And that, in any case, Aitmatov's tragedy is no cause for pessimism but, on the contrary, for confidence that the Soviet people will reach their goals.

Assuring readers that he was entering the argument, rather than simply taking note of the opinions, for the sake of encouraging serious literary discussion, Aitmatov himself answered his critics. Most, he said, had missed the principal message of the myth of Horned Deer-Mother, which concerned one of the world's most pressing contemporary problems: man's need to establish a harmonious relationship with nature, 'to preserve the wealth and beauty of the world around us'. The exposure of senseless killing teaches man to hate cruelty and to appreciate his responsibilities before mankind and his own conscience.

Having made this fresh point, Aitmatov hammered home several far more obvious ones. The purpose of myths, he said, is to instil collective feelings of striving for the good, and for this, not only 'positive' tales with happy endings are effective. There is nothing 'inconsolable' in a tale which provokes an abhorrence of evil in its readers. Nor, to cite just one example, was Shakespeare guilty of pessimism in allowing Juliet to die. For although a tragedy in life, her death, through its effect on the spectator, is something quite different in art. The lad's death is indeed 'The White Steamship's' most controversial element, but the fierce refusal of some readers—and critics too—to reconcile themselves to it showed that they completely misunderstood its artistic meaning. "There is indeed a solution, but it lies beyond the limits of 'paper', in the reader's heart."

To the critic who had complained that after the killing of Horned Deer-Mother 'nothing is left on earth except darkness and the butcher Orozkul', Aitmatov answered: "No my dear man, 'the reader' is still left." To the reader who suggested that he should have arrested Orozkul, awarded grandfather Momun a pension and sent the lad to a boarding school, he replied patiently that life was not always like that. To a host of readers and critics who complained that another ending was possible, he answered that his was inevitable because 'good, in the person of the lad, turned out to be incompatible with evil in the person of Orozkul—and since the lad was a lad' he could fight Orozkul only by withdrawing. "Momun's passive kindness collapsed and the lad's irreconcilability to evil stays with him, he swims away with it . . . and if he finds a haven in the reader's heart, this is his strength, not his 'inconsolableness'. Frankly, I'm proud of my lad."

Aitmatov wrote column after column to explain that the novel is not a tale of evil defeating good or of pessimism about the future, and that while art must indeed serve as an inspiration for happiness, optimism and love of life, it sometimes must do this by plunging man into profound meditation, arousing powerful feelings of compassion and protest against evil.

> Many of mankind's radiant dreams have come true and more will be realised. History is moving towards betterment. But this doesn't mean that evil has been fully defeated . . . It would be good if people under various kinds of pressures and burdens never compromised with their conscience or capitulated to evil. Alas, however, evidently mankind must make considerable further efforts to free all people from these 'weaknesses'.

One may wonder why these self-evident points were made at such length and with such fervour. Since Aitmatov's critics themselves insisted that the tale be judged 'on a wide historical background', outsiders may feel entitled to speculate about the context of the debate. Surely the arguments about pessimism, tragedy, the function of literature and rightness of judging each work in terms of overall Soviet goals, represented real issues in themselves; but they may also have served as vehicles for more specific, therefore sharper, political questions touched upon by implication.

One such implication is very broad: Orozkul is not only a cruel man, but a Stalinist. One need not know that he actually admired Stalin himself (this is the meaning of his reference to 'the good old days' when 'heads flew') to understand that his outlook, methods and especially his attitude to authority is in the pattern of those who brought grief to Russia. His type exists in every country of course, but it has had unusual success in Russia, and by the very act of placing this vicious creature in a position of authority, not to speak of 'winning', Aitmatov has posed the question of the power enjoyed by the Orozkuls in contemporary Russia's bureaucracy. From other sources, it is known that they in fact exercise a great deal of power, and that higher authorities are extremely displeased by any public reference to it. Why do such people have control over other people? the lad asks. Why do people put up with such men?

This suggests an even more sensitive issue. Grandfather Momun is a good and kind man, as the Russian people are generally good and kind. He (like they?) breaks his back, knuckles under to everyone and has only his fairy-tales to believe in. "As always, Momun submitted" — moreover, to a ruthless authority whose notion of civilisation is far below his own inherent instincts. But in a sense, all his 'passive kindness', as Aitmatov describes it, comes to nothing because it 'collapses' before Orozkul's petty terror. Surely this tragedy pertains to much more than one Soviet family.

"You want to cry out: he couldn't have, Grandfather Momun couldn't have killed the maral," wrote one critic. "He couldn't because ... kindness and good were in him, and he couldn't not rise up in rebellion, not cross his sword of justice with evil in mortal combat." But Momun 'did' rise up in rebellion at the river—and lost.

A more relevant observation was made by a 'Novy Mir' critic shortly before, while discussing Mikhail Bulgakov, an extremely important writer who fared badly under Stalin and has yet to be given his rightful place in Soviet letters. The critic pointed out that Bulgakov considered cowardice 'the most terrible vice' and condemned it without mercy or indulgence "because he knew that people who make evil their intention are less dangerous than those who seem prepared to embrace good, but are faint-hearted and pluckless. Fear ... makes good men into blind instruments of maliciousness ... [and] ... cowardice is an extreme manifestation of inner submissiveness of a subjugated spirit."

This is not the place for an analysis of Soviet history, but it seems obvious that the whole of it would have been vastly different if not for the sometimes puzzling submissiveness of the Russian people in the face of the hateful authority of the Orozkuls who staffed the dictatorship. Surely it is far-fetched to imagine that Aitmatov intended a precise parallel between Momun's fate and that of the Soviet people. Surely the novel's character types exist everywhere, and the story 'works' as such because its dramatic and psychological elements are universal.[1] Nevertheless, in the tragedy of the Soviet Union at the hands of Orozkuls and the regime's great reluctance to examine this aspect of the past and its legacy in the present, 'The White Steamship' has a special native significance. Young Moscow intellectuals, in any case, talked of it in these terms and supposed that some of the ire of its critics was provoked by the underlying implications, and sharpened by their own unwillingness to take up such themes openly.

---

[1] In a private letter, Aitmatov himself recently drew attention to the resemblance between his lad and the protagonist of the film 'Kes'. "I find much in common," he wrote, "in the fates of these two boys, one English and the other Kirghiz."

The discussion of 'The White Steamship' was summed up by 'Literary Gazette', the newspaper in which the bulk of the articles had appeared. No one had tried to prove that Aitmatov had written the wrong ending, the editors explained, but merely that it was not justified by the novel's own development. Moreover, the editors added, that the theme of the fight for the good was indeed 'somewhat muffled' in the story. Thus the newspaper made peace, not without stretching the facts to suit its own argument, while emphasising the discussion's benefit to literary public opinion. And lest it be imagined that Aitmatov suffered because of 'The White Steamship's' unconventionality or the controversies it provoked, it should be reported that there are no signs of diminishment in his official favour. In 1971, he was working on a film script about lorry drivers who spend their lives on treacherous mountain roads and raw construction sites. He continued to be given prominent places in the literary and popular press, including 'Literary Gazette' and 'Pravda', where he championed his artistic ideas with uncommon bluntness. As before, he combined attacks on Western literary and political trends with appeals for betterment in his own country; defended socialist realism as the only viable contemporary school while drawing attention to Russian masters, such as Dostoyevsky, whose insights go far beyond those associated with any single school, nation or ideology; called upon literature to face its highest responsibilities to humanity – stimulating compassion for hardship and suffering – and castigated authors with a 'hack attitude towards literary work'.

Pleas to raise the standards of Soviet literature underlay many of his public statements, together with criticism of 'some authors who write with extraordinary facility in all genres and all forms, invariably addressing mankind and Man with a capital "M" in pompous pretentiousness and in their own names'. In the Soviet context – and in the indirect language of literary and political discussions – this is surely an appeal for writers to do their own work rather than the armchair pundit's or propagandist's. Soviet literature must be educative and uplifting – but in the way great literature always has been, not through vapid generalisations about the advantages of socialism, the heroism of the Soviet people and the progress of mankind. Socialist realism has a job to do in the Party's service, but can do it only by creating real characters in real conflict, rather than the stereotyped figures (Party secretaries or plant foremen, for example) in hackneyed situations (righting a local wrong or overcoming a difficult production problem) in which so many good-overcomes-evil Soviet stories are couched.

These concerns are hardly new to Aitmatov; he has spoken on many platforms for many years about the insufficiency of ideological rectitude or good intentions as a basis of fiction, without the traditional literary ingredients of talent and hard work. After 'The White Steamship', however, his statements seemed to have attained a greater maturity and confidence. Confidence, that is, in what is needed to be done rather than in his own ability to do it, for it is a sign of his maturation that he is cautious about the latter. "I did not come to the conviction at once," he wrote recently, "but now have no doubts: a literary protagonist cannot be without his problems. Whether a positive hero or negative, he cannot be without conflicts." Aitmatov's emphasis indicates he is moving still farther from oversimplified Soviet fiction, in which good and bad are personified rather as in the era of the least subtle, therefore most tedious, Hollywood Westerns. How to treat conflict in protagonists has plunged Aitmatov into creative thought.

> These days, I am like a pilot who has temporarily lost his bearings while landing in an unfamiliar place. I am groping my way through clouds ... towards the ground and towards life; I circle over them in thought, trying to make sense of the human affairs, actions and fate which comprise the kernel of historic events and daily happenings, trying to ... concentrate and fix my attention on what is most important ... that is, on people's characters and life situations which would enable me to say something new and significant about our time and our life ...

Although there is no evidence that Aitmatov is any less eager to 'serve the Party with truth and faith', than as a young writer, this expression of uncertainty (together with the warning, in his reply to 'The White Steamship's' critics, to avoid 'risky generalisations about "the history of mankind"') is indication enough of his understanding that the most fervent ideological commitment solves few artistic problems.

Several weeks later, at the Fifth Congress of Soviet Writers in June 1971, Aitmatov was chosen to speak from the tribune, and took the occasion to defend 'complicated' young writers from attacks and to deplore several aspects of Soviet literature. "Our greatest misfortune," he said, "... is the abundance of mediocrity, of that deceptive outward show as when there is more foam than liquid. But for some reason I find it hard to remember when we had a serious, professional discussion about this in a large gathering of writers. Actually, at multitudinous meetings and conferences, in the capital and the provinces, at all small and large literary forums, the problems of artistic craftsmanship are discussed only after everything else."

Aitmatov also restated, even more clearly than before, his conviction of the need for tragedy in Soviet literature despite the 'diverse notions' about it that 'we sometimes encounter'. "It seems to me," he told the six thousand delegates, "that the time has come for extensive discussions of our conceptions, comprehension and experience of the nature of the tragic in art, of our understanding of tragedy in Soviet literature. This is a part of life as it exists, and cannot be ignored. Tragedy will be with man forever, just as happiness, consciousness and creativity. It is a part of his life and his environment." *Moscow intellectuals felt that Aitmatov was one of a handful of interesting speakers (Yevtushenko was another) in a Congress otherwise not distinguished for its originality of thought or expression, and this strengthened their admiration for him and expectation of his promise. A perceptive critic remarked privately that his talk stood out from the run-of-the-mill speeches like his stories from the bulk of Soviet fiction.* "He's growing every day," said the young man. "Sometimes I'm amazed at how far he's come, and how much he's been able to get away with. 'The White Steamship' was tonic for us all."

Like many of Aitmatov's admirers, this critic feels that his non-Russian nationality helps him as some blacks are helped, in a sense perversely, in America: he is allowed more liberty than a Russian because cultural authorities lean over backwards not to be accused of suppressing a member of a minority group. This argument is sometimes dismissed, but there is wide agreement among intellectuals that Aitmatov has become a force in Soviet literature, and much is expected of him.

DATE DUE

FEB 23 1998			
FEB 20 REC'D			
DEC 18 1998			
SEP 10 REC'D			

Demco, Inc. 38-293